DESTINY

PRAISE FOR THE GIFTEDVERSE

This one kept me interested from the very beginning. With a lot of drama, intrigue and some magic, it's fast paced and entertaining.

— DOODLE BUG

…This trilogy is action packed from start to finish with love and loss along the way… From first book to last, the Owens women will keep you fascinated.

— SUNNI

Packed with excitement, danger, adventure and a rollercoaster ride of emotions. I couldn't put it down until I finished it!..

— CYNDEE MARLING

Wow. That is all I can say about this book. It kept me on my toes waiting to find out what came next. It was well-written with a lot of character and world building.

— SARAH COLEMAN

THE GIFTEDVERSE SERIES

In reading Order:

The Owens Chronicles

Prophecy

Destiny

Legacy

The Gifted Chronicles

First Life

Second Chance

Third Eye

Companion Volumes

Annabelle

Etta

Find out more at

www.giftedverse.com

DESTINY

THE OWENS CHRONICLES
BOOK TWO

AMANDA LYNN PETRIN

CHAPTER ONE

The light I was using to read the Chronicles in the cargo train went out once it got dark outside. Silly if you asked me, but I guess they weren't used to people riding with the merchandise in the cargo crates. I put the book back in my bag and tried to get some sleep, but my head was spinning.

I started the summer off full of excitement, ready to get away from the house I grew up in and start a new life in college. I never expected to end it on the run for my life with Embry and Gabriel.

My heart felt like it hadn't slowed down since Donovan found us and broke it into a million pieces. I tried not to think about Sam, my surrogate big brother, but he was the reason I wasn't sleeping like Gifted knights in shining armor. Every time I closed my eyes, all I could see was Sam. How I left him on the cold, hard asphalt to bleed out and be discarded somewhere, probably never to be found. How I let him die.

Letting it happen would have been bad enough, but I went one step further and caused his death. Donovan wasn't going to kill Sam until I said no. Until I fought back, knowing that someone like Sam would pay the price.

I shook my head to get the images out, but Embry must have been watching me rather than sleeping like I thought. "You should get some sleep," he told me.

"I'm not tired," I lied, struggling to keep my eyes open.

"You're safe for now Lucy. We won't let anything happen to you." He gave me a reassuring smile, but I knew he couldn't promise that. He and Gabriel would both give their lives to protect me, but they were out of their league. "Come here."

"I'm not really..." I tried to come up with a lie about how fine I was.

"Come here," he repeated, his Italian accent more pronounced when he was tired. I crawled over to where he was sitting and leaned into him while he wrapped his arms around me. "I've got you." He kissed the top of my head. While Gabriel had always kept his distance, at least emotionally, Embry had been a constant source of love and support.

"I know," I assured him. It just wasn't enough.

"Donovan is weak right now. Every time we come back, it takes a while for our Gifts to return at full strength. Everyone who was following because of him has to be recruited all over. We can go to the plantation, get some supplies, and find somewhere safe so we can be prepared to face him when he comes back." I knew the only way he would let me fight Donovan was over his dead body, but that was still a likely scenario.

The compartment was quiet, other than Gabriel's occasional snore. I tried to concentrate on that, but the longer we sat in the dark, the more I felt the pain and fear I was burying rise up.

"What did the Chronicles say?" Embry nodded to the book of stories from my ancestors, pulling me from my thoughts.

"I didn't get very far," I admitted. "I think Beth is why Grams made soul cakes for Halloween, though." One of Beth's first entries was a recipe for them. "And why we jumped into the creek to celebrate the solstice," I ventured. It sounded like something she would do.

"Beth had some superstitions." I could hear the smile in Embry's voice.

"She didn't grow up at the plantation like the rest of us. Or the manor. She moved to New Orleans when she was little, and never came back. From what I gather, that kind of stuff is accepted there."

"It's definitely a place where magic feels possible," he agreed.

"Says the guy who's turning three-hundred-and-forty-seven." He and Gabriel both looked like they were in their early twenties, but I now knew that they were Gifted, and had spent the past few centuries protecting my family.

"The whimsical kind of magic that amazes and amuses, but doesn't harm or curse," Embry elaborated.

"The kind that doesn't actually exist?" I fished for stories.

"There has to be a balance somewhere," he argued.

I didn't remember falling asleep, but I woke up to Embry gently shaking me.

"Wake up, *bambolina*," he used one of his Italian terms of endearment for me.

"What's wrong?" I felt my heart racing. The darkness was gone, and the sun was shining in through the door Gabriel wrenched open, but my fear was ever-present.

"Nothing's wrong. We're just getting off before the end of the line," Embry assured me with a smile that didn't quite meet his eyes.

"What station?" I asked, putting my backpack on, and slowly waking up.

"We can't wait for the station. People would see us getting off, we'd have to explain ourselves—"

"Then how are we getting off?" One look at them told me the answer, but I was not ready to accept it.

"We jump." Gabriel gave me a smile. It was his genuine, excited smile, which only made it worse.

. . .

GABRIEL WENT FIRST. He lowered himself until he was almost touching the grass, then used his supernatural speed to hit the ground running. I wouldn't say that I was panicked, but it was more than Embry reassuringly touching my arms that got me to actually jump. I didn't like Embry using his Gift to manipulate my feelings, but it was better than the alternative of him pushing me out a moving train against my will. As it was, I landed in Gabriel's arms as softly as could be expected, with my eyes shut tight and possibly not breathing. I could feel Gabriel's heart pounding next to mind as I tried to calm down.

"I've got you," Gabriel whispered, no longer running. "I'll always catch you," he promised, waiting a little longer before cautiously putting me down.

"That wasn't so bad, was it?" he asked without taking his arm off me until we walked a few steps with my legs holding me up, rather than buckling from the shock.

"I never want to do that again," I argued. Embry had landed on the grass a dozen feet ahead of us, so I went over to make sure he was okay.

"There'll be a bruise in the morning, but I'm fine," Embry assured me, brushing a twig out of his sandy blonde hair.

"Which way is home?" I looked from one to the other. I couldn't even tell you which state we were in.

"This way." Embry put his arm around me and confidently steered us in the direction the train came from.

"I'LL HAVE the three-egg western omelet with sausage, bacon, and ham on the side. Whole wheat toast is fine. Hash browns, beans, and seasonal fruit would be great, with an order of pancakes and black coffee," Gabriel ordered from the diner's waitress while I stared at him in disbelief. He was occasionally hungry enough for an egg, a piece of toast, or a bit of oatmeal, but his usual breakfast consisted of black coffee with nothing else.

"I'll have the same, but French toast instead of the pancakes, and espresso rather than coffee," Embry told the waitress, who raised her eyes to him in surprise. She probably assumed, like me, that Gabriel had ordered for the table.

"I'll just have…" My stomach growled as if I hadn't eaten in days. I looked to the guys and remembered we were starving because none of us had eaten anything but the protein bars from my backpack since before we got to the motel. Plus, they both fought in multiple battles, died, and came back to life. "I'll have pancakes with bananas and Nutella, and all the meats they're having." I chose to forego the fruit and granola yogurt bowl for something more substantial.

"Coming right up." The waitress gave us a smile before moving on to her next table. There was a man sitting alone at it with four stacks of pancakes, each with different toppings. We weren't the first customers to order large amounts of food.

"I didn't even realize how hungry I am." I had to look away when I got the urge to stick my fork into one of the man's pancakes and eat it.

"It comes in waves," Embry explained, as his stomach made the same growl mine had.

"How are we getting to Boston from here?" The diner menu told me we were in Missouri, which was still a ways from home.

"I saw a used car dealership down the road. Depending on how legit he is, that could be an option." Embry tried to make it sound like a fun prospect, but I had no interest in riding in a car from a shady salesman that would likely fall apart on us.

"We could also hitchhike across the country if staying under the radar is more important than staying alive," I said in an optimistic way that had Embry shaking his head at me. "I thought we had a breather now, which is why we're going home. If they're still looking for us and ready to pounce, I'm not going anywhere near my family." The guilty feeling in the pit of my stomach intensified when I mentioned Deanna and Clara, Sam's wife, and daughter. How could I call them 'family' when I sacrificed Sam so the bad guys wouldn't get me?

"I would never take you in a car that wasn't completely safe, *Tesoro*," Embry assured me. "But we don't want to be obvious about where we are, or where we're going."

Gabriel's main focus was on the other patrons in the greasy spoon. Aside from the man with the mountains of pancakes, the diner had two other occupied tables. One with a man in a suit reading the newspaper and drinking black coffee, then another with a young family dressed like they came from church. The parents looked exhausted, while the children were as excited about their brunch as I would be for Disney World.

"Can I have bananas and strawberries on my pancakes?" the little boy asked.

"And blueberries!" his younger sister exclaimed.

"You can have whatever your heart desires," the dad said, ruffling the little girl's hair.

I got lost watching them, thinking how Sam would never be able to ruffle Clara's hair like that again. Because of me, the only happy family I had ever known was broken.

"If you could go anywhere in the world, where would you choose?"

I was surprised when it was Gabriel who asked such a silly question, but I saw concern when I brought my attention back to our table. He'd been watching me watch the family.

"Italy," I gave my standard response. "Everywhere." I shrugged, my heart no longer in it. I still wanted to see the world, but home was the first place I thought of. My main problem was that home wasn't home anymore.

"I'm sure we'll knock a few places off your list." Embry gave me a smile as the waitress showed up with three plates that all went to Gabriel. She came back multiple times to bring two plates for me, three for Embry, and some sides she left in the middle of the table.

"Could we go to a library at some point?" I asked, trying to swallow the ginormous bite I took.

"Missing homework?" Embry raised an eyebrow at me.

"Research. If I only read what they wrote, I'll never know more than they knew." I swallowed and took a piece of bacon from the plates in the middle.

"I doubt any of it will be in a library," Gabriel argued.

"Libraries have internet," I pointed out as the mother's phone from the other table went off with the Imperial March. I was momentarily distracted by how cute it was that the little boy hummed along. Once she answered, it only took him a few notes to turn it into a song from Mary Poppins. "And there are biblical references and Latin words I want to confirm," I came back to our conversation as if I hadn't spaced out.

"My Latin is excellent," Embry volunteered. "But we can still check out a library at some point."

The conversation took a lull while we savored our meals. I had my doubts about the hole-in-the-wall diner we encountered by the train tracks, but the pancakes were big and fluffy, the bananas were perfectly ripe, and they were generous with the Nutella.

"Ready to hit the road?" Embry asked once our plates were mostly empty, and he finished his third espresso.

"I'll use the restroom, then I'm ready to go." I stretched as I stood, picked up my backpack with the Chronicles inside, and handed it to Embry to watch while I was gone.

"We'll get the bill," Gabriel told me, motioning the waitress over.

· · ·

THE WASHROOM WAS BETTER than I expected. It was old, stained, and falling apart, but you could tell that it had been cleaned recently.

I was washing my hands when the young mother from the other table walked in and headed straight for the other sink.

"Is that one empty too?" she asked me when her soap was empty. She held her hands out like they were covered in something gross and sticky.

"Nope, it's all yours," I told her with a smile, heading to the paper towel dispenser to dry my hands.

"You're nicer than the last one."

Something about her voice made the hairs on the back of my neck perk up.

"The last what?" I turned around, looked into her eyes for the first time, and knew exactly what made me uneasy. "You're one of them." She was wearing blue contacts, but they only made the darkness underneath stick out. "How did you find us?"

"Some wounds heal, but they always leave a scar." She kept her eyes on me as she moved closer.

"What do you want?"

I took a step back, only there was nothing but wall behind me. Not even a window to escape from.

"What I want is to get back to my grandkids and enjoy a nice Sunday brunch." Like Embry and Gabriel, she was clearly a lot older than she looked. "But Donovan doesn't believe in coincidences, so the two of us in the same room is apparently too good of an opportunity to pass up on." She sounded bitter. "Everyone's gotta have something to live for." She sighed, giving me the impression that she didn't think too highly of the Big Bad's quest.

"What's yours?" I asked, my voice shaky. "Have you done it yet?" I scoured the room but didn't see anything I could use as a weapon. Everything was either bolted down, or innocuous. I could try some of the self-defense Caleb taught me when we were hiding on the island, but this woman was almost a foot taller than me, and looked like she could be a personal trainer.

"That is so cute. Worried you'll hurt me so bad I won't come back?" she mocked me.

"We can't all be villains intent on destroying humanity." I tried to hit a nerve.

"Don't let my grandbabies fool you. I've killed infants with my bare hands and still sleep soundly every night."

"Lucky you." I swallowed, taking one last look around. I still felt guilty for the Gifted I strangled so I could escape at the gas station. And the guy the house evaporated at the plantation, even if he was trying to kill me at the time.

"Listen, we can do this the easy way, or I can carry you out in a bag. It's up to you." She stood with her hand on her hip.

"You can't hurt me," I said with a conviction I didn't feel. I knew my death was what they all wanted, since my heart was an ingredient in a ritual they had to perform, but I was pretty sure Donovan's master – the *real* Big Bad – had to be the one to do it.

"I can't kill you," she conceded. "But there are lots of ways to get you to him without taking all the life out of you."

"My friends are right outside. If I scream, they'll—"

"They'll die," she said simply, with a lot more confidence than I had earlier. "And I'm not sure if they'll come back from this." She touched the sink to her left without taking her eyes off me. The stained ceramic went grey as she turned it to stone.

A chill went through my entire body. On the bright side, unless she could reverse it, turning my heart to stone meant no one could use it to complete the ritual.

I saw her take a step towards me and froze. I closed my eyes so I wouldn't see it coming and put my hands up, as if that could protect me.

I waited for the blow, but it didn't come. There was a gust of wind and a loud bang, then nothing but a faint ringing in my ears and tingling in my palms.

When I opened my eyes, the woman was gone.

The sink slowly turned back to white ceramic and my heart dropped into my stomach. I stood there, frozen, before looking down at my hands. They still felt tingly, but looked completely normal, without a scratch on them. I cautiously took a step forward, to see if the woman was hiding somewhere, but the sink reverting to its former self told me I wouldn't find her. The only thing different from before I closed my eyes was a small pile of what looked like sand on the floor where the woman had stood.

"Is everything okay?"

"What happened?"

Embry and Gabriel burst into the washroom, probably expecting an explosion based on the noise. All they got was me, standing alone and in shock.

"We need to get out of here," I said, snapping myself out of it. There was an explanation for what happened, I just couldn't think of it with the ringing in my head.

"Are you alone?" Gabriel looked around to see what had me so frazzled.

"Yes." I looked to the pile of sand that was most likely her ashes.

Embry and Gabriel were looking for answers, but I knew it was only a matter of time before the woman's husband came to see what was going on, at which point he would either finish her mission, or call the cops on me.

I ignored their questioning looks and went to leave the washroom, relieved when Embry beat me to the door and opened it for me. I was half-expecting an army of Donovan's men to be waiting for us, knowing what I did and ready to exact their revenge. Instead, the hallway leading to the washrooms was empty.

"Let's go this way," I suggested once I saw that Embry already had my bag on his shoulder.

I brought us to a back door that opened to a row of dumpsters. I could see the road off to my right, but every other direction had tall grass covered in dew. It would be great to hide in, but we wouldn't get very far, at least not very fast. There was a car parked on the other side of the dumpsters, probably older than me, covered in rust, with a duct-taped plastic sheet covering one of the windows. It was falling apart, but would serve our purpose as long as we ditched it before the owner reported it stolen and the cops caught up with us. I was about to make sure one of the guys could hotwire it when I heard the unmistakable hissing of a large bus using its brakes. "Do you have cash?" I asked instead, hurrying towards the road. There was a guy my age walking around the front of a city bus, wearing headphones and looking down at his feet instead of the world around him.

I looked back towards the diner and saw the husband was no longer sitting at his table, but standing in the middle of the restaurant, looking upset. We did not have time to argue over not having bus fare.

"I think I have a twenty." Embry fished it out of his pocket. They followed me into the road but looked at me with confusion and fear. I wondered if my face was as red as it felt, if they could see it. Maybe not what happened, but that I caused something terrible, without meaning to.

Luckily the bus driver, a plump woman with tight curls, waited for us to get on.

"You're new, child," she said, looking me up and down as I walked by.

For the first time today, I looked down at myself. It was

hidden by the table at the diner, but our adventures from last night were now on full display. Gabriel's jacket covered most of Sam's blood, but the mud was everywhere.

We took our seats, and the bus took off. I looked back at the diner through the window and saw my victim's husband rush through the doors to look around outside. I could almost feel his anger as he kicked the ground and took another look in each direction before going back inside. I let out the breath of relief and sat back in my chair. He wasn't coming after us. At least not for now.

THE GUYS WAITED for the adrenaline to die down and for my breathing to go back to normal before they both looked at me with all their worried intensity.

"What happened in there?" Gabriel's tone demanded an answer.

"The woman who came in after me, she was Gifted. One of Donovan's more willing participants." I swallowed and saw Gabriel clench his fists.

"Why didn't you scream, or call for us?" Embry asked.

"She said she would kill you," I said simply. "I believed her. She touched the sink and it turned to stone," I cut them off before they could defend their fighting skills against a lone assailant.

"But she left you?" Embry was confused.

"The sinks were normal when we came in," Gabriel pointed out.

"She died," I whispered.

"How?" I felt like the guilt must be written all over my face, but they were expecting an answer.

"She was coming at me, but I couldn't find anything to stop her with, so I closed my eyes and raised my hands and…and pouf."

"And pouf?" Gabriel pressed.

"There was something that sounded like an explosion and when I opened my eyes, she was gone. The sink went back to normal."

"The pile of sand," Embry realized.

"Ash," Gabriel corrected. Neither of them took their eyes off me.

"Looks like you've got powers," Embry said with a sad smile, sounding worried more than anything. He wrapped his arm around my shaking frame while I kept my hands glued to my sides, terrified of what they might do.

CHAPTER TWO

We didn't get off the bus until the end of the line, at which point our driver told us of some nearby hotels, and showers we could use. We got the hint.

"Child." She stopped me when I was on the steps, with the guys on the ground, clocking our surroundings. "I don't know if they're the bad situation, or if they took you away from it, but there's a women's shelter two blocks that way. Tony will be on the bench, ready to step in if they give you trouble." The look in her eyes told me she had been there before.

"Thank you." I was touched by her concern. "But they're the ones keeping me safe."

"It's always open," she called after me when I stepped off.

"Where to?" I asked the guys, looking around the busy street. If I had managed to convince someone to bring me here last summer, I would have admired the Gateway Arch that towered over their skyscrapers and spent hours watching old boats pass us by on the Mississippi River. As it was, the hustle and bustle of the city put me on edge, with every person we crossed a potential threat to be avoided and feared.

Embry and Gabriel gave each other a look, then reached a decision with head tilts and shoulder shrugs.

"This way," Embry ushered me over once they were on the move. We went from the main streets to side streets until we reached back alleys that, while creepy, made me feel less out of place.

"Tip Top Body Shop?" I read when we stopped. Gabriel stayed with me while Embry went to check if it was open.

"This was Eli's place, once upon a time. It shut down over a decade ago, but as far as we know, he still owns it, and it's really old, so they can't tear it down."

"Eli as in the guy who lost an ear and was half-deaf for decades?" They'd mentioned the name once before. There was a blue circle plaque beside the door, so I went closer to check it out. "He was from here? Established 1905 by Elias Nettle, oldest garage and gas station in Missouri," I read out loud.

"In his first life and everything," Gabriel agreed. "I think by the end he was pretending to be Elias Nettle the Eighth or something. Family-run since the day it opened." He gave a rare smile.

"Why did it close?"

"His line died out." Gabriel's tone was simple, but I could tell from his face that it was anything but.

"You were close?"

"We all were."

I made a mental note to ask Embry, who was always more forthcoming, before he motioned us over to the now-open front door.

"You've done this a lot?" I guessed.

"Eli had a lot of qualities, but he was never going to be the one to help you in the middle of the night."

"Because of his ear?" It might be hard to hear if you were sleeping on your only ear.

"Even before that." I got another tiny smile from Gabriel.

"He just wouldn't come?" After Terrence and Caleb who self-lessly housed us while we were on the run, risking their lives in the process...I had trouble picturing a friend of theirs that selfish.

"He couldn't hear you over his own snoring. It was horrendous. The phone, knocking, sirens...nothing got through to him once he fell asleep. He would wake up every morning at six, without an alarm, but good luck if you needed him before then," Embry shared.

"This is how you would sneak into his shop in the middle of the night?"

"Exactly."

"We once spent hours trying to wake him up after we kidnapped him for his bachelor party. We were not as careful as we should have been in transporting him, and we started drinking long before we tried to wake him," Gabriel admitted. I couldn't help but wonder if his we included Embry, and they'd actually hung out together and had fun, not just to protect my family.

The inside looked like an abandoned garage. Usually, when a business closes, the owners liquidate their inventory, selling whatever they can to recoup their costs. They would also go through the normal steps and procedures to close down a business, at least on a daily level. This place looked more like everyone got up mid-workday and left. There was a car up on the pillars with two tires off, tools and paperwork all over, a desk calendar with future appointments... The only signs that it wasn't a working garage were the lights being off, and the inches of dust coating every surface. When Gabriel said Eli's line died out, I got the feeling it was all at once.

"We can stay here tonight and head out in the morning," Embry suggested.

"We can't go home anymore," I pointed out.

"Where do you want to go?"

"Far away from Boston." I was horrified at the idea of going anywhere near the people I loved. "You said we had a breather now, that we were safe for a while, but Donovan knew we were at the diner. He called that woman and told her I was there."

"That phone call could have been anything," Gabriel argued.

"But it wasn't. Maybe everyone out there knows what I look like, but she wouldn't have come after me if Donovan didn't make her."

"I'm sorry," Embry said like he had failed me, yet again.

"I don't understand how they keep finding us." Gabriel was angry. "We knew they would come to the plantation, but we were careful after that. The safe house, the motel…we did everything right."

"Wounds heal but they sometimes leave a scar," I admitted. "I asked her and that's what she told me." I shrugged, not sure what she meant by it. I had a lot of emotional scars that were never going to heal, but physically I was fine.

"That doesn't make any sense," Embry voiced what I was thinking, then looked to Gabriel, to see if he had any ideas.

"It wasn't like they followed us. We ditched our phones, we traveled in a chicken coop, and…you died," I said when it hit me, but they both looked at me like I was crazy.

"We both died, but that wouldn't help them find us. It's not like sparks go up and light the sky," Embry argued.

"She said some wounds heal, but they always leave a scar. That's true for normal people, but when you guys come back, the wounds are gone, right?"

"Like it never happened," they both agreed.

"You once told me you always buzz at the airport because there's shrapnel in your shoulder from—"

"The wound healed, but the scar is on the inside. They put something in me when they found us at the plantation," Gabriel realized.

My excitement at figuring it out died when I understood the implications. "That's my theory, but it sounds too high-tech for him, so it's probably not..."

"Don't underestimate him. He's not alone. Even if he is as clueless as you would expect from someone his age, which I don't think is the case, his followers are kids your age. Some of them probably work at Google or Facebook," Embry warned.

"We need to take it out before we leave here." Gabriel gave Embry a look and a subtle nod in my direction.

"Later tonight," Embry agreed.

"We can take care of it later, because we need supplies and a clean environment to do it in, but from now on, I'm not being the kid who has to be protected from the truth. I know you want to protect me, so you can keep all the evil people away, but I will be right there when Embry digs around inside you to get it out," I warned Gabriel.

"Not offering to do the honors?" He gave me a sad smile.

"I would if there was no one else," I assured him. "I'll hold your hand and help in any way I can, but I would rather not cause you pain if I can help it."

"Luckily for you, Embry enjoys it."

Embry rolled his eyes, not dignifying the accusation with a response.

"Let's get you cleaned up," he said instead, showing me to the apartment above the garage.

I WAS EXPECTING a messy bachelor pad with stuff lying out as if the owners left in a hurry, like the garage below, but it was empty. Or I should say devoid of anything personal. There were fresh sheets on top of the night table and neatly folded towels on the sink's counter, along with a pack of hotel toiletries. There were no photos, no knick-knacks, absolutely nothing to even hint at who Eli was.

I took the shampoo, conditioner, and body wash, then put the water as hot as it would go, which still left a lot to be desired. At first, I let the water rinse off the dark brown crust, telling myself it was only mud, determined to keep it together. The blood was caked onto me, so it was indistinguishable from the crusted mud, until I looked at the stained water circling the drain.

It brought me back to the plantation, to watching Gabriel's blood swim down the drain, but at least he came back. I was traumatized then, but this was so much worse. Sam was gone. Forever.

Once I was as clean as could be on the outside, I put on a pair of shorts and a t-shirt, with Gabriel's jacket on top. The chill wasn't letting me go.

I FOUND Embry in the kitchen, making mac and cheese. All I could smell was cheese and butter.

"We also have a healthy salad," Embry assured me without turning away from the pot he was stirring.

"Thank you." I took a seat and filled my plate with salad. His 'healthy' salad had a dressing made of olive oil, balsamic vinegar, and honey over a bed of mixed greens, cashews, and raisins.

"Is it ready?" Gabriel came in with his shirt off, looking like he'd been lifting weights, with his earbuds in and sweat glistening.

"Pretty much." Embry turned around and saw his attire. "Trying to look pretty for me?" he teased.

"I don't know how butchered I'll be by the time you're done with me. This might be the last time I can do anything," Gabriel defended himself.

"Until the next time you die," I said dryly.

"This smells delicious. Thank you," Gabriel said after a slight pause, where we all sat in silence. I didn't mean to be bitter and make things unpleasant, I just couldn't help it.

"It's perfect," I seconded.

"Gabriel also picked up some dessert." Embry cautiously smiled once we were done with the meal. Gabriel went up to the freezer and came back with cookie dough ice cream.

"Will the Big Bad be intimidated if I weigh three-hundred pounds?"

"No, but we feel better about ourselves when we supply you with comfort foods, and convince ourselves they make you feel better."

"All better." I gave them a smile and took a spoonful of ice cream.

THE GUYS GAVE each other looks again, then both got up and walked out of the room. They looked at me with confusion when I followed them.

"No more keeping things from me, remember?" I pointed out, then walked past them into a room with a table they'd somehow already set up for surgery. There was a garbage bag under the ledge of it to catch the blood, and a tray with the instruments Embry would need.

Gabriel shrugged at my determination, then took his place on the table.

Embry looked at me, then to Gabriel, and sighed.

"Hold him down." He let me take part. He took out a scalpel and hand sanitizer, then moved with purpose. I wanted to ask what he was doing with this stuff, but I had to prove myself if I wanted them to stop leaving me out. By the time I figured out how I was going to control Gabriel without getting in the way, Embry had spread the sanitizer and brought the scalpel to his skin.

"You're going in blind?" I asked, shocked.

"Do you have an ultrasound machine lying around?" Gabriel countered, like I was the one being ridiculous.

"No anesthesia or anything?" This was going a lot faster than I expected. Embry pressed hard enough on the scalpel that he drew blood, but didn't cut yet.

To answer my question, Gabriel took out a bottle of Jack Daniels and downed a few gulps of liquid courage. "Go," he told Embry, who nodded to me.

I did my best to hold Gabriel down, but he was used to pain, and mostly gritted his teeth through it. He barely moved while Embry dug around inside him, but I kept one arm and my body weight across his chest, in case. My other hand found his and held it throughout the procedure, although I'm not sure if that was more for him or for me.

My biggest fear was that I was wrong, and Embry wouldn't find anything inside him. That he would poke around and cause immeasurable pain before giving up and bringing us back to square one. Fortunately for my guilt, after some very pointed looks from Gabriel, Embry eventually pulled out a tiny black device. If that didn't confirm my theory enough, there was a flashing red light at the end of it.

"We got it," Embry told his patient, holding it up so Gabriel could see. He handed it to him before grabbing a needle and thread to stitch him up.

"Our first clue." Gabriel showed the tiniest bit of enthusiasm before finally passing out from what must be unimaginable pain.

"That's not normal thread," I pointed out, a poor attempt at distracting myself. It looked a lot thicker than the one Mrs. Boyd used on my clothes, once upon a time. "You had this lying around?"

"We left the garage as is, maybe as a shrine, maybe because it was hard, but Eli asked us to turn the apartment into a refuge.

In our line of work, that requires a very elaborate first aid kit," Embry explained.

"You should splurge on an ultrasound machine next time." I got a smile as he stitched Gabriel's skin back together. "What happened downstairs?" I felt him tense up.

"Nothing." I got the feeling Embry was just as close to Eli as Gabriel. "Eli's Gift was to see the future. Sometimes he could make a vision happen, other times they came to him unbidden. He would share if he thought it could help you, but didn't see the point in hurting people before bad things happened. There was a man who didn't like what he saw and kept trying to convince Eli to change it. One day, the man went to the market and shot Eli's wife, as well as his three remaining descendants. Eli was working in the garage when he heard, so he ordered everyone out, threw a chair into the apartment window and never came back."

CHAPTER THREE

We didn't leave in the morning as planned. Gabriel spent the next twenty-four hours or so going in and out of a comatose-like sleep. Embry insisted the wound would heal and he would be fine, but we didn't have real painkillers, so Gabriel spent a lot of the time he wasn't knocked out asking us to kill him so he could come back without the pain.

Embry's face did not betray any emotion as he convinced Gabriel to go back to sleep, but I had to turn away and bite my lip every time he woke up. I couldn't stand the agony in his voice, but I wasn't going to cry over it in front of him. I once suggested that maybe we should consider listening and putting him out of his misery. That's when Embry decided I could only stay in the room with Gabriel if I promised not to say another word about it, or interact with Gabriel when he was like that.

I spent most of my time holding Gabriel's hand, wishing this wasn't so painfully familiar, but I also spent time looking into the tracker.

We assumed they knew where we were by now, even though we were pretty sure we deactivated the tracker when the red light went out. Embry let me use an old laptop from the garage that weighed twenty pounds and still used dial-up to do some research.

"Any leads?" Embry asked, drawing my attention away from Gabriel, who moaned in his sleep. I bit down on my lip and tried not to react.

"There's a serial number on it, so I did some googling, and it was apparently sold as a way to track wild animals for conservation projects, using this website." I brought the laptop over so he could see the map. "It only gets updated every few hours, but that's us right there." I pointed to the screen. All the other dots were in clumps, but there were none anywhere near us.

"Could we use this to see where they are? Maybe know ahead of time when they're coming for us?" he asked.

"I have no idea," I admitted. "I think we could probably figure out where they are when they're actively tracking him, but…I was able to figure out this much because it was easy, but even when they're on TV shows talking about tracing IP addresses and all that tech stuff, I have no idea what they're talking about. Which means that even if it is something we could do, it will take a long time for me to figure out how to do it."

"And I thought I had completely embraced the twenty-first century when I let you convince me to buy a smartphone." He gave a half-hearted smile as we heard Gabriel waking up again.

"I think you need to use it for more than phone calls to qualify," I teased. It was easier than watching Gabriel in pain.

"The OnStar woman taught me how to use the maps too," he boasted before I gave in and turned over to Gabriel.

He was obviously still in pain, but he asked for water instead of a mercy killing, so I happily obliged.

By that evening, Gabriel was getting up and slowly moving around, so I made dinner. It wasn't that Embry and I hadn't been eating while Gabriel was out, we just didn't make it a priority. I was also pretty sure that getting cut into and slowly repairing yourself, cell by cell, might make you as hungry as dying and coming back to life.

I made us grilled cheese sandwiches with bacon and apples. I was checking to make sure the cheese was melted when Gabriel walked in, his shirt unbuttoned so I could see the white bandage on his chest.

"You're up!" I was unable to contain my enthusiasm, but I stopped myself from taking him in for a hug like I wanted to. I had to assume the wound was still painful, and the last thing I wanted to do was cause him more pain.

"I've had worse." He saw where my eyes went, and only winced a little when he sat down.

"I don't ever want to have to see you like that again," I admitted, putting the food on a plate in front of him.

"Embry said you found out how they've been tracking us. Does that mean we know where they are too?"

"We don't, but I found a hacker who insists they can find anything and anyone, so that's an option." Even if I didn't have the necessary computer skills, I was still reluctant to get anyone else involved. I didn't trust people at this point, and I couldn't have another death on my conscience.

"Do you mean a tracker?" he asked.

"No, like a computer hacker."

"We're relying on computers now?" Gabriel raised an eyebrow at me.

"It's how they've been finding us."

"Touché." He bit into the grilled cheese and closed his eyes for a second, savoring it. "Maybe instead of letting some stranger behind a screen keep tabs on them, you could do it with a spell," he suggested.

"I'm pretty sure you need magical powers to do that," I turned him down. He'd said it like he was trying to be helpful, but Embry had also tried to bring up what happened in the bathroom. I was severely in denial and not interested.

"Luce—"

I didn't have to shoot down his next argument, because we heard glass breaking from downstairs before he could get it out. We looked at each other in silence, both of us aware Embry was in the bedroom, and this was the last location the bad guys had for us.

"Get your bag and the books. Now," he whispered to me before Embry came into the kitchen, only partially dressed after his shower, but holding some kind of axe, with a spare one for Gabriel.

"Get her to the car, I'll hold them off as long as I can," was the last thing I heard Embry say before I rounded the corner into the bedroom.

I shoved all my clothes into the backpack, with the Chronicles and the Book of Shadows, then went to find Gabriel in the kitchen.

"Come on, we'll take the fire escape." Embry must have gone downstairs, because it sounded like a battle was raging.

GABRIEL OPENED THE WINDOW, though it clearly hurt him, and climbed onto the fire escape. It was the kind where the ladder didn't go all the way down; you had to hang on it and wait for it to lower itself.

"Are you okay?" I asked Gabriel when it got stuck and he had to use his body's momentum to propel it down.

"It's easier than getting it down when you're at the bottom," he assured me, but I could see he was in pain, and when the movement brought his shirt open, his white bandage was turning red.

The ladder finally budged and made a clinking sound when it hit the asphalt below. Gabriel waited at the bottom for me, but as I grabbed on to the rusted railing to follow, I was pulled back. The air was knocked out of my lungs as I hit the ground.

"There she is." The man who spoke looked like he was at least seven feet tall and didn't loosen his death grip on me. The world started spinning, so I tried to pry his fingers away from my throat, but there was nothing there. *Not now*, I lamented as the alley disappeared, and I was brought into a memory from one of my ancestors.

"I assure you sir, I have nothing. No money..."

I was Annabelle, on the side of the road, trying to appear calm and reason with the man who found her there, alone. I could feel how afraid she was, but there was also surprise. She was someone who had traveled great distances before, and never been so accosted. Then again, she'd never been without a male companion. Her father was with her on the crossing to America, and every time she ventured away from home in the years since then, Gabriel or Embry were always by her side. Men looked at women on their own completely different than when they were properly accompanied.

"That ain't true, lass. You've always got something we want," the old man said with a toothless smile. It did nothing to dissuade me from my first impression, that he was planning on kidnapping and possibly having his way with her.

"Please sir, I mean no trouble..." Annabelle pleaded with her eyes, which had worked in the past. She then looked around to see if there was anyone there who could help her, or at least ensure she was relatively safe from being taken away. All I saw were three younger, well-built working men, whose smiles didn't allow any confusion. These were definitely not nice men, and they were not going to help her.

"Where are you heading sweetheart?" one of the new arrivals asked, sizing her up.

"My husband will be along shortly. I'm sure he would be happy to help you with whatever..." she tried to sound as convincing as she

could, but I could hear her voice faltering. Lying wouldn't work any better than the pleading had.

"You don't got no ring." One of them smiled, knowing he had her. No one was coming to our rescue.

She looked away from the man who was making her uncomfortable to see if there was a branch on the ground or a rock, anything she could use to defend herself. I saw nothing.

"Darling, I'm terribly sorry I'm late. I promise it will never happen again. Have these gentlemen been helping you out?"

At first it was just a voice with a British accent, like Annabelle's father's, until she looked up and I saw a dashing gentleman who smiled as he extended his arm for her to take. He could be another brigand, looking to take advantage of her like the other men, but right now he was the lesser of two evils, and she didn't have a choice.

"I was telling them you were on your way." She tried to steady her voice and sound like she believed it. "We should get going if we want to get home before dark." The other men's faces dropped, angry they lost their plaything, but her good Samaritan was a foot taller than their tallest, and looked strong and sturdy.

"We should," he agreed, so she accepted his arm and walked with him. She kept her head high and exuded confidence, while inside she was gripped by terror. She was waiting until she was far enough away from those men to thank this one and leave, at which point we would find out if he actually saved her, or took her for himself.

"I apologize for the impropriety, but I didn't get the impression that you knew those men," he said as we walked along, his voice soothing. "I'm Henry." He put his hand on top of hers like Gabriel used to, making her blush. Soon enough, her heartbeat slowed, and I was more and more convinced he was not going to kill her.

"No, thank you so terribly much for saving me. At first, it was just the old man, but then they were everywhere," she admitted, trying to shake away the fear they left her with. "I'm Annabelle."

"A pleasure," he assured her. "There are some exceptions, but I do believe most of us gentlemen would prefer to save the damsel in

distress rather than be the ones distressing her. Not that you were in distress, of course."

"Of course not." She smiled at him. "I believe I can find my way home from here."

"As you wish." He released her, so she was free to go. "I don't mean to impose, but it would put my mind at ease if I could walk with you until you truly were at your home, or at least no longer roaming the countryside on your own. Beautiful women should never wander on their own in foreign lands."

"I'm afraid it's only me," she admitted. "I probably shouldn't tell that to someone I just met, but you'll never stop following me if you wait for me to be properly accompanied."

"I wouldn't mind." He looked into her eyes, and I could feel her cheeks redden as she swallowed hard. He was obviously flirting, but unlike the other gentlemen, he was not making her uneasy. If it weren't for the fact that her heart and love life were in shambles, she would have been receptive to his advances. "That is very independent of you." He went back to being polite, looking ahead instead of at us.

"Or incredibly foolish," she acknowledged.

"There's a fine line between foolishness and bravery. For example, I can't tell if it is rather brave of me or completely foolish to ask if I could call on you tomorrow."

I watched him nervously rub his fingertips together while Annabelle debated his proposition in her mind. Her first instinct was to apologize and tell him she was taken. It seemed like less of a lie than the truth, that although her heart belonged entirely to another, she was currently without attachment. Hadn't she come here in an attempt to move on with her life? To find someone who was neither Gabriel, nor Embry, and try to be happy.

"I believe it would be both foolish and brave of you," she said as he was about to turn away again. "Lucky for you, I am choosing to reward bravery today. I would love for you to call on me." I could feel her heart break a little as she said it, but I knew she wasn't going to end up with Gabriel, and I liked Henry so far.

"Then it shall be my pleasure." He smiled and she tried to dismiss the sinking feeling in the pit of her stomach, the voice that screamed for her to stay away, that he was not the one she should be with.

"This is me." She stopped at the gate to her little cottage.

"My task is done. I bid you a wonderful evening and look forward to our next encounter." He tipped his hat before continuing along the path, as Annabelle let herself into the house that still felt like someone else's, though it had nearly been a year...

I WOKE up to find the man who'd been holding me was now unconscious at my side, with Gabriel in the kitchen, fighting. I knew the guys would want me to keep going and find a car or something, but I had no means of contacting them, didn't know where we were going, and was convinced I would fare better with them than alone.

Everyone was preoccupied with their own battles, so I was able to climb back into the apartment through the window, carrying a broom from the balcony like a weapon.

"What do you think you're doing?" Embry asked, knocking one of the assailants out with the blunt end of his ax.

"Helping."

"You need to figure out how to control those things," Gabriel said of my tendency to relive memories from my ancestors. He wasn't happy with me, in the way Mrs. Boyd would get upset when I snuck out the window and she couldn't find me.

"You're preaching to the choir." I sighed and shoved my broom into someone's stomach, letting Gabriel knock him out once the man doubled over.

A woman who'd been on the floor got up and rushed at me. My first instinct was to put my hands out to somehow brace myself or stop her, but I barely lifted them when I remembered what happened last time, and felt the tingling start. I froze, paralyzed with the thought of killing someone else, so Embry hit her on the temple with his elbow. He shot me a look I had never seen on him before, at least not directed at me, where his nostrils flared, before I hurriedly picked up my broom handle. I stood at the ready, like I hadn't been about to let that woman hurt me so I wouldn't have to relive her death in my nightmares.

Soon, there were five bodies on the ground, with the three of us still standing. "They won't be out long," Embry warned, exchanging a look with Gabriel. All I could tell was that they were worried, and we needed to leave fast. My guess was that more people were coming, and Gabriel was nowhere near ready for another fight. He barely made it through this one.

Embry went first to get the ladder back down to the street, and I went second to ensure no one would grab me from behind. Once the three of us were clear, Embry took off through the alley, gently guiding me while keeping a brisk pace. We rounded three corners and I felt like we were in a maze before we finally stopped in front of a residential garage. It was white once, but the paint was so cracked that it was more of a moldy brown now.

"Eli kept a getaway car?" I asked when Gabriel took the keys out of his pocket rather than breaking a window to get in.

"He wanted it to be a refuge, but sometimes the bad gets in."

CHAPTER FOUR

We drove to a train station, at which point Embry used cash to buy three tickets. There were half a dozen scheduled stops along the way, but Florida was our final destination. He did it as three separate transactions, with three different tellers, at least fifteen minutes apart.

"What's in Florida, other than Disney?" I asked Embry while we waited for them to call us for boarding.

"I don't know." He shrugged his shoulders before casually looking around, as opposed to Gabriel, who was actively scouring the room for threats.

"We're going to wing it?" I was pretty sure that wasn't in their DNA.

"There will be a stop somewhere along the way where we will get off so someone else can take our places. Three people who could pass for us, at least from a distance. They are the ones who will enjoy Florida," he said under his breath.

"But you won't tell me where we're going?"

"Nope." He crossed his arms.

"Way to make me feel like a child," I reproached, pulling Gabriel's jacket tighter around me. I could see how floating in a grownup's jacket made my statement ironic, but I was eighteen years old, not six.

"Compared to me you are very much a child," he pointed out. "If it makes you feel any better, I'm not telling Gabriel either. You'll both see when we get there," he assured me before they called us to board our first train to Lincoln, Nebraska.

THE PASSENGER TRAIN was an extreme upgrade from the cargo crates we rode to Missouri in. We switched trains three times before taking an overnight train to Georgia. I lasted that long without taking a nap, but once we were in our own cabin, with the lull of the train, I couldn't resist anymore and finally surrendered to the exhaustion. Gabriel was the only one of us who got enough sleep over the past few days, but I doubt any of it was restful.

I tried to get comfortable with my head against the window, thinking how this train was a lot faster than the old steam ones, but there was still the same flow that carried you to sleep…

"GABRIEL," Rosalind said, her breath catching in her chest when she saw him walking over. I could tell she hadn't seen him in a while, but he had definitely crossed her mind many times.

He paused before masking a look of disappointment, that she might not have noticed, but I did. "Rosalind." He took her hand and kissed it.

"It's been a while."

Gabriel turned quickly, and Rosalind followed his gaze to see Embry in the doorway with a little girl, Molly, who rushed right over to jump into Gabriel's arms.

It melted Rosalind's heart to see the way Gabriel held her daughter close, but she tried to hide it from him. Gabriel didn't even look at us before turning back to the doorway.

"Embry," he said through gritted teeth, nodding his head.

"I understand now. About Annabelle." Rosie looked back to Embry.

"I'm glad you found each other." Gabriel forced a smile for us, but it disappeared the moment he looked away.

"We're not together," Embry told him as if it meant something, but Gabriel didn't react.

"How long are you here for?" Rosalind asked, but it was Molly's big grey eyes looking up at him that held his attention.

"Maybe a week or so. I was in town and wanted to make sure the both of you were okay. Now that you know."

"If Embry hadn't come and told me the truth, what would your pretense have been?" Rosie unashamedly called him on his lie, getting a smile in return.

"I might have developed a limp or injured myself on the way." He smiled in spite of himself, with a softness she found as unexpected as I did.

"I would have seen right through it," she said with a smile before Molly tugged on his sleeve and he agreed to accompany her to the meadow. Rosie nodded to let him know it was okay. Her heart dropped to watch him walk away, but Molly's joy at being reunited with her friend was everything to her.

THE SCENERY CHANGED but I was still Rosalind. She was walking towards the stables that used to be behind the plantation, long before I was born. Gabriel was there, taking care of some horses, looking like he'd been there a while, long enough to get comfortable.

"Thank you." Rosalind put her hand out so the horse could sniff it. She didn't react to the way the horse's breath tickled, but she avoided looking into Gabriel's eyes.

"What for?" He continued to brush the horse's mane.

"Molly. Losing Roger was very difficult on her, and I haven't seen her smile so much as she does when she is with you."

"She's a brilliant little girl. It's my pleasure," he assured her. He was polite, but distant.

"Gabriel..." She gave up pretenses, stopped petting the horse and turned to him. "I know you've seen how Embry looks at me, and I want you to know that I do not return his affections. Even before you came back, I couldn't love him, because I loved my husband until the day I was sure he was not coming back, and then...then I fell for you." She took a step closer to him, but he put his hands out, as if to stop her, and took a step back.

"Rosalind..."

"Gabriel..." She looked right into his eyes, staring him down like I did sometimes, but I wouldn't have been able to stay there with the way her heart was pounding in her chest. "You can't pretend there isn't something between us. You can't bury it by avoiding me, and—"

"I see her," he cut her off, then looked away so he wouldn't see the pain in her eyes, but it was clear in her voice as she asked, "What?"

He brought her to a bench and took her hand in his, sending heat and shivers to her spine.

"You look exactly like Annabelle. The clothes are different, but other than that, as far as looks are concerned, the two of you are identical. Every time I see you, my heart breaks because I have to actively remind myself that you are not the woman I am in love with. And I want you to be happy, and safe, and I want to protect you. I wish I could love you like you want me to, but I can't, because I am still in love with the girl I met when I was a boy, who stole my heart and never gave it back. You look like her, and for that I am sorry, but I love Annabelle, not what she looked like." I could tell he didn't say it to be mean, that he just wanted her to understand that any looks of affection he accidentally sent her way were simply him forgetting he lost Annabelle, but I could feel her heart breaking when he said it.

"Gabriel..." She wanted to argue, to tell him it couldn't simply be because she looked like Annabelle, that he obviously had genuine feelings for her...

"You can't talk me out of this. You should accept Embry's advances, find happiness." His words cut into her heart like a knife.

"I wasn't going to," she said, her anger the only reason she was able

to hide how much it hurt. "I understand that I can't talk you into loving me, but I am not a lovesick child. And you can't talk me into loving Embry instead of you either."

"Then what did you want to say?" He looked heartbroken as well.

"Don't leave because I made the mistake of falling for you. I promise that I will never bring it up again, if you could just stay." She tried to appear strong, and I gave her so much credit for that, but her pain and vulnerability were screaming at him.

"That would not be a good idea. For either of us." He was apologetic. Even if he didn't love her in that way, I don't think he wasn't unaffected either.

"But it's what's best for Molly. I understand if you have to leave, I have no claim on you, but I'm a mother first, and that girl, who is my world, she loves you. And I would hate to think I was the one who cost her the only person since her father who can make her laugh like that."

He looked into her eyes, but all I could hear was her broken heart pounding in my ears. He considered it for the longest time, what felt like an eternity.

"I'll stay," he agreed. "I'll stay for Molly."

"Thank you." She gave him a sad smile before getting up and going about her day as if nothing had happened...

I woke up to find Gabriel watching me, with a kindness he didn't normally show, especially not during the day. He usually kept his distance, but got more vulnerable at night, when he possibly thought I wouldn't remember what he said to me. I had been longing for another one of these late-night conversations, ever since the night at the plantation when I wore the lace dress that reminded him of Annabelle, and he told me about his brother.

"When you look at me, do you see me, or do you see Annabelle?" I asked, snuggling into Embry, who was asleep beside me. I knew I looked like her, but what he said to Rosalind made me wonder.

"Do you want the truth, or a bedtime story with a happy ending?" He reverted to his carefree, bored self, but I didn't feel like he was trying to protect me from an ugly truth, more like he was the one who didn't want to admit to it.

"The truth." I closed my eyes a bit like I was falling back to sleep, so he would put his guard down. It was wrong of me to manipulate him like that, and I knew it, but it was also mean of him to be really nice to me and tell me things when he thought it wasn't registering.

"I always saw her," he admitted. "When I woke up in Rosalind's arms, I thought I died and went to heaven, to Annabelle...but then I saw the differences. Some were big, others were small, but none of them were Belle. I never got used to it. Every time I saw them, I would think 'Annabelle' then remind myself that it couldn't be." I could hear the pain in his words like I had seen on his face in the memory. "It was like losing her all over again. Every single time," he shared.

I opened my eyes a crack and saw he was talking to himself now, assuming I was asleep. I kept my eyes closed and concentrated on the rhythmic breathing that fooled him all those years ago in the East Wing.

I wanted to apologize for the pain it caused him to look at me. I knew he still loved her, but I didn't realize he still forgot, even after all these lifetimes without her.

I thought he was done, but his next words shocked me so much I forgot to breathe. Not just breathing slow to pretend like I was sleeping, but breathing altogether.

"Until you. I came for your eighteenth birthday, and you ran to me, so relieved and happy to see me, wearing this pink dress, and my first thought was 'Lucy'. Not Annabelle. And it broke my heart." He paused a moment, during which I felt his gaze on me. "I couldn't be near you anymore after that. Not until all of this." He sighed before getting up and telling Embry he would go make sure everything was good in the other compartments.

IT WAS ONLY when Gabriel shut the compartment door behind him that I realized I was holding my breath. I kept my eyes closed, but wasn't fooling anyone.

"You weren't asleep," Embry reproached now that we were alone.

"Neither were you." I tried to turn it on him. "He doesn't talk when he knows I'm awake," I relented.

"Be careful with him Luce," he warned before we heard Gabriel making his way back. "Get some sleep," he recommended, with a kiss to the top of my head.

I looked at him, remembered how hurt he was watching Rosie choose Gabriel, and did as I was told.

I cuddled into Embry and tried to fall back asleep, but it was hard when the two of them were talking. Eventually, Embry kept watch while Gabriel got some rest, but my mind was too stuck on what he said to sleep. What did he mean that seeing me broke his heart?

I opened my eyes, thinking maybe I could convince Embry to talk it out with me in the hallway, but once my eyes were open, they immediately locked with Gabriel's, who was on the other seat, facing me, his eyes open and staring at me. I rationalized it by reminding myself it was their job to protect me, but he didn't stop when he saw me looking. We kept our eyes locked, without acknowledging each other or moving, until sleep finally made my lids drop and I drifted off to sleep.

WHEN EMBRY SHOOK ME AWAKE, the train was still moving, but there were three extra people in the compartment with us. The two men had the same hair colors as Embry and Gabriel, both dressed in black. The girl, however, looked nothing like me. She had a mess of curly brown hair, like mine, but she wore it up in a bun and was almost a foot taller than me. Her dress either came from my closet at the manor, or she happened to buy the exact same style.

"This is Tristan, Benjamin, and Delia," Embry made the introductions. I remembered Delia's name from the chalkboards at Caleb's safe house, but no one ever mentioned the other two.

"It's nice to meet you, Lucy." Tristan, the one with dark hair like Gabriel's, had a warm and welcoming smile, while Benjamin looked...not quite miserable, but like this was one of the last things he wanted to be doing right now.

"We've heard a lot about you." My decoy was older than me, but not by much. There was something about her eyes, even without the darkness, that told me she had lived many, many lives.

"All of it terrible." Embry smiled, but Delia shook her head at him.

"He brags about you constantly," she told me. "And you're an Owens, you have no choice but to be kind, selfless, and perfect." She rolled her eyes, but was smiling at me.

"Is that something we're known for?" I asked.

"According to these guys." She nodded to Embry, then to Gabriel.

"You should wear your hair down," I told her. I didn't feel so perfect, and wasn't looking forward to letting the Owens reputation down.

"We know their disguises won't hold if they see them up close," Embry defended.

"If it's someone new, they might not know exactly what I look like, but I think they'll all know about my birthmark," I pointed out. It was the whole reason they were hunting me.

Embry nodded, but Delia turned around to show me her

neck. It was a near-perfect replica of my crescent moon birth-mark, complete with the freckles in the middle that looked like stars. "Etta was going by memory when she drew it, but I think it'll hold up if it isn't someone who knew one of you." She got a sad look on her face. I had yet to meet Etta, whose husband Caleb had housed us at the beginning of the summer, but I knew she was incredibly close to Cassandra, the version of me from the eighteen-hundreds.

"Which one?" I asked, touching the back of my neck as if I could feel what it looked like.

"Mostly Cass, but I think I've met all of them, except for Annabelle." She looked to Gabriel for confirmation.

He nodded, so Tristan, his decoy, asked, "We're just going to Florida and chilling, right? There's nothing you need us to do once we get there?"

"That's it. You can work on your surf or meet Goofy. We just need enough time for them to lose us," Embry assured him.

"Oh, we brought these for you." Tristan took a bunch of brightly colored garments out of his backpack and handed some to each of us.

"You're enjoying this too much," Gabriel warned, putting a Hawaiian shirt over his black t-shirt.

"I would enjoy it a lot more if I had a camera to take pictures back to everyone else," Tristan argued.

"These don't go together," I said of the long black coat and baseball cap they brought me. The guys were used to dressing in black, but I was usually in colors.

"We're not aiming for fashion, just something you wouldn't usually wear," Embry assured me as the train slowed to pull into the station.

"Thank you." Gabriel took Delia in for a hug, while Embry shook the guys' hands.

"We would love to have you at Rosehill when this is all over. We miss you," Delia told him.

· · ·

I FOLLOWED Embry and Gabriel out of the compartment and through the busy train, careful to keep my head down.

"They're Gifted, right?" I verified, knowing they would be hunted if their disguises passed the test, possibly killed if they didn't.

"Of course," Embry assured me.

"And they haven't done what they were supposed to do?"

"We wouldn't let them do this if they had." Gabriel guided me to an exit.

I nodded, thinking that I should have been raised by people like that, instead of Sam, Deanna and Clara.

WE WENT to a beat-up Volkswagen in the parking lot, that Embry somehow had the keys for. It was so old that he had to actually put the key into the lock and turn it to unlock the doors, then lean across to unlock Gabriel's door, and the one behind him for me.

"Can you tell me where we're going now?" I asked, taking the middle seat.

"Not too far," Embry said, giving no actual indication of time or place

"And we're currently in…" I looked around for a sign since I hadn't been paying attention at the station.

"Right now, we're in Atlanta."

I tried to pretend this was a road trip vacation so I could forget every horrible thing that happened in the past few days.

CHAPTER FIVE

I t was two fast food stops, one gas station, and approximately seven hours before we arrived in a very secluded neighborhood of New Orleans.

There were gates and wide-open spaces, but not a lot of houses. Embry drove up to a villa surrounded by fields and stables on one side, with trees and swampland on the other. The house wasn't nearly as big as the ones I grew up in, but it was at least two to three times the size of a normal house.

"Who lives here?" I asked, looking around at the beautiful expanse of land. It was like a cross between an Italian villa and New Orleans charm.

"I do." Embry got out of the car and looked around at the property. "At least sometimes," he amended.

"How long have you had it?" I wondered if it was a new acquisition, or part of his life I knew nothing about.

"Since 1922." He looked at the house like he could see the first time he saw it, with the memories alive in front of him. They made him smile, but it was a sad smile. Beth, the last copy of Annabelle before me, lived in the early nineteen-hundreds and grew up in New Orleans. It wasn't a leap to think she might have something to do with it.

"There is absolutely no security here," Gabriel declared after a few minutes of observation, unimpressed.

"It wasn't designed for something like this, but we can manage," Embry assured him. "If anything gets out of hand, we can send Lucy to the panic room."

"You put a panic room in this house?" Gabriel raised his eyebrows.

"I made a fireproof room to protect things." There was a finality to the way he said it that dissuaded Gabriel from any further arguments about the location.

"Your plan is to lock me in your bunker with your favorite things?" I verified.

"If things get out of hand." Embry smiled at me, so I rolled my eyes before smiling back at him. I knew better than to complain about tight spaces or not being able to go outside. Others had given up way more than that to keep me safe. Plus, I grew up exploring a manor with secret passageways that I sometimes got lost in. I even had my own bunker I'd locked myself in before, not that I wanted to repeat that. But I didn't want the guys to keep shutting me out whenever things got dangerous.

EMBRY TOOK a key from under a flowerpot and let us into the foyer, which wasn't as dark and dusty as I expected.

"A flowerpot? Seriously?" I asked him. Gabriel was fuming, but kept it inside for the moment.

"Locks are easy to break if you really want to get in." Embry shrugged before bringing us to the kitchen.

"When's the last time you were here?" There were eggs and milk in the fridge, along with other very perishable items. The pool in the backyard was spotless, with the jets running, and all the bushes perfectly manicured.

"I want to say months, but I think years would be more accurate." He saw my look and elaborated, "I have someone who takes care of the place, and he knew I was coming."

"How?" Gabriel perked up as if ready to relocate me immediately.

"You're not the only one with top-secret messaging systems," Embry defended.

"What's in here?" I continued the tour in an effort to diffuse the situation.

The room in front of me looked oddly familiar. There was an oak table covered in books and papers, an antique chair with extra cushions, an old gramophone…it looked like Embry hadn't changed anything in the room since he got the house.

"This is storage; we don't have to go in." Embry hurried in front of me and shut the door before walking us through the laundry room, wine cellar, and his study.

Next, he brought us up the stairs.

"Don't worry about these rooms," he said of the first two, that he didn't even glance at as we walked by. "This is a bathroom, and some spare rooms," he said of the next ones. "And if anything happens, this is how you get to the panic room."

He brought us through the master bedroom and pressed his hand to the wall to reveal a walk-in closet. It would have been a fashion enthusiast's paradise, but other than one rack in the corner, there weren't any clothes.

"Is this where you hide all the corpses?" I asked of the trunks.

"Just treasures." He still had that sad smile. "I even have some first editions if you get bored." He pointed to an ornate bookshelf, filled with incredibly old, yet pristine volumes. He had all the works of Jane Austen, J.D. Salinger, Ernest Hemingway, Shakespeare, some Italian playwrights, and a bunch of books whose authors I never even heard of. There were four books at the bottom that looked brand new compared to the others, all written by Laurel Haynes.

"Hopefully this is my first and last time in here," I told him, walking out. I touched the carvings in the bed frame and everything disappeared…

I COULD TELL *I was in the same room, but while Embry's closet looked dark and a bit like a shrine, this one was warm. I knew I was Beth, even before I caught a glimpse of her in the mirror, but her eyes were focused on the reflection of the closet, rather than on herself. She was in a red silk negligee, with her hair cut a few inches below her ears. She looked so happy. Happier than I had seen any of the girls in any of the memories.*

"When are you coming to bed?" she called to the closet, where I could hear someone rummaging around. This must be the house she shared with her husband, David. It explained why the room downstairs was so familiar; it was the room Beth had been researching the prophecy in.

"Got it!" I was shocked to hear Embry's voice exclaim, before he came into the bedroom, positively triumphant.

"You have less than ten pieces of clothing in there. What took you so long to find?" she asked, stretching around in the bed.

"This." He hopped into the king-sized bed beside her, a small velvet box in his hands.

"You spoil me," she said it like he should stop, but she was smiling. She kept her eyes on him, not even noticing the gift box.

"You deserve it." Embry gave me a kiss on the forehead. I don't think I had ever seen him so happy, or with so little clothes on, which was slightly awkward. I was used to Sam prancing around in his boxers back home, so it wasn't a big deal, but if things went any further, we would have a problem. "Happy Anniversary." He kissed her shoulder. Luckily, I wasn't the one controlling her, because it tickled, and I would have burst out laughing.

Beth, on the other hand, chose happy tears as her response to the kiss and the ring with four stones that she found in the box. Birth stones by the looks of them, but I didn't know enough to know which was which, and she closed the box before I got a good look.

"These have been the happiest five years of my life."

She kissed him on the lips. It was incredibly strange to be kissing him like this, when I couldn't control my actions, and could feel what she felt for him. I knew what was coming and willed myself to come out of the memory, but I was saved when knocking on the door made them stop.

"Come in munchkin," Embry called, laughing.

A little girl ran into the room and climbed into the bed between me and Embry. I recognized her as an older version of Helen from my last Beth memory.

"I had a nightmare," she said, cuddling into Embry. "There was a monster in my closet."

"Do you want me to go make sure everything is safe?" he offered.

"No Daddy! He'll hurt you!" Helen looked up at him, eyes wide. "Can I sleep with you and mommy tonight? Please?" she begged.

"This is why we needed the bigger bed." Beth smiled before they lifted the covers so Helen could crawl under them. Beth and Embry looked into each other's eyes over Helen's head, holding hands, and fell asleep like that.

WHEN I CAME BACK to the present, Gabriel was holding me up and Embry's eyes were locked on mine, like in the memory. Only instead of love, I saw his fear over what I might have seen.

"Oh my God, did I…" I remembered what I was doing in this memory, and my tendency to act them out.

"No, you passed out. We didn't know if it was a memory or…" I felt flushed, but I wasn't sure if it was from what happened in the memory, or the way Gabriel kept his arms around me, even though I was more than capable of holding myself up.

"It was just a memory." I swallowed, exchanging a look with Embry, while Gabriel looked at me with concern.

"From who? What happened in it?" He was ready for clues.

I fumbled for an answer, but was saved from lying when an old man with white hair and kind eyes walked in.

"I was hoping it was you," he said, his voice full of southern hospitality.

"Charlie." Embry relaxed his shoulders and rushed over to the newcomer. He took the man in for a hug like they were old friends. "This is the man who watches over the place when I'm gone."

"I had help this time," Charlie assured me. "Eric!" he called into the hallway.

"Yes grandpa?" a voice drifted up the stairs.

"Come on up," Charlie called.

Eric was tall and tan with golden locks and his grandfather's kind eyes, only the blue in them was piercing rather than calming like Charlie's. He looked strong in a rugged way, like he helped run the stables and was used to lifting barrels of hay.

"You remember Embry, and his friend Gabriel." Charlie paused for them to shake hands. "And this must be Lucy." He reached over and shook my hand with an endearing smile.

"Was it Beth?" I figured Charlie was yet another Gifted who knew my ancestors.

"I'm old, but not that old," he said with a wink. "Your grandmother and I used to run around and ride the horses here before she moved away. She became a treasured pen pal who sent a lot of pictures after that."

"I didn't know she had any friends," I said before realizing how that sounded. "I mean, outside of the house. She mostly kept to herself."

"She wasn't always like that," he told me.

"They were little troublemakers," Embry cut in. It was weird to picture him running after younger versions of Charlie and my grandmother.

"I believe I have more than made up for it." Charlie didn't argue with Embry's assessment. "We came over to make sure it was you and to invite you to dinner. It's just a little barbecue, but—"

"We would love to."

Embry surprised me with his acceptance, and by the looks of it, Gabriel as well.

"I'll give you a moment to get settled in, but we'll be in the yard when you're ready." Charlie smiled at each of us before leading his grandson out. Eric shot me a smile and I could feel myself blushing, which was not something I was used to.

"You think it's wise to leave the house and parade her around?" Gabriel asked Embry once our guests were gone.

"We share the land and no one else comes out here," Embry defended. "She's as safe there as she is here, and Charlie makes the best crawfish I've ever had. Ever."

Gabriel still didn't look happy, but he went to change out of his colorful outfit and came downstairs in dark jeans and a black t-shirt.

I changed into my last clean outfit, which happened to be a dress. In hindsight, I should have packed more adventure clothes and less vacation ones. I made a mental note to do laundry when we got back, so I would have something to wear in the morning.

Embry was the last to come down, wearing black pants and a button-down shirt, that he rolled up at the sleeves.

"Off we go," he said with a smile that reached his eyes. The best description I had for his mood was that he was finally home after a really long and hard journey, so he delighted in, and appreciated, every inch of it.

WE WALKED out the kitchen patio doors and went past the pool, to one of those long picnic tables. Twenty people could sit at it comfortably without touching elbows.

"Blanquette de Limoux." Embry walked over to where Charlie was working over a huge pot and handed him a bottle of wine.

"Thank you." Charlie looked touched.

"Can I get you something to drink?" Eric came out of nowhere and offered, making me jump slightly.

"What are you having?" I asked of the amber drink in his hand.

"Iced tea. Well, my grandma's version. It's a combination of sweet tea and lemonade with a hint of secret ingredients."

"Secret ingredients?" I raised an eyebrow, but he just smiled. "I'll try one."

"Excellent choice," he told me before going over to a pitcher in a bed of ice and pouring me a glass, which he topped with a slice of lemon. I watched him with curiosity, but Gabriel watched like he was making sure no one slipped anything into my drink.

"Do we trust them?" I asked Gabriel in a whisper, leaning closer to him.

"I trust Charlie." He didn't take his eyes off Eric.

"Eat, eat," Charlie insisted, even though he was still busy cooking. I was fine with waiting, but Eric brought me the iced tea and led me to the food table.

"Have you been to the South before?" he asked me.

I considered it before saying, "Not really."

He didn't need to know about our recent adventures, running for my life through a tropical jungle and passing the border from Mexico on a truck filled with poultry. It wasn't like I was introduced to any new foods, at least none that looked like the spread in front of us.

"Do you like seafood?"

"I do…" I tilted my head and bit my bottom lip, trying to figure out if I should trust him, which made him laugh.

"Everything is amazing, so you can try it all and let me tell you what it is after, or I can tell you now and you might miss out." Eric shrugged, showing a clear preference for the first option.

"Those are my only choices?"

"They are." He was apologetic, even if it was mockingly so.

"In that case let's try it all." I laughed in spite of myself. Tonight was in such a crazy contrast to everything we had been through lately, that none of it felt real.

Eric scooped up things that were deep fried, some that were boiled, and a bunch of sides I thought I recognized, but on closer inspection, did not. There were none of the barbecue staples like hot dogs and hamburgers. Instead, there was gumbo, jambalaya, po-boys, and various types of crawfish. My favorite was the deep-fried crawfish with a spicy mayo sauce, until I tried the jambalaya. It was a smorgasbord of sausage, seafood, rice, and the perfect amount of heat. Everything was delicious.

I WAS LAUGHING along with Eric's story about a rogue crab when Sam's face flashed in front of me, so proud when he finally caught the lobster Clara briefly adopted as a pet. For a second, I had forgotten that I was being hunted, that I caused my brother's death. I was just a girl at a crawfish boil with a cute boy, trying new things.

"You okay?" Eric looked concerned, but he kept his smile.

"I'm fine." I made an effort to smile back, hoping he didn't see how fake it was.

"How long are you guys staying here?"

"I have no idea," I admitted.

"Are you from New England also?"

"Boston," I agreed. "Have you ever been?"

"I checked out MIT my senior year. And stopped by Harvard for fun." He smiled at the mention of the Ivy League.

"Where did you end up going?"

"I'm at Louisiana State." He shrugged. "Where do you go?"

"I was supposed to start Harvard in September, but I had to defer." I tried to make it sound unimportant rather than admit that lifechanging events made me doubt if I would even survive to go to college at all.

"Harvard, huh? That's fancy."

"I had a boring and sheltered childhood." It was how I usually explained away my good grades, or lack of friends, but now I could see there was nothing boring about the way I grew up. I would give anything to go back to that sheltered life instead of this one, where I see the world from different hiding places, and lose the people I care about.

"Mine was noisy," he said after considering it. "I have three brothers and three sisters."

"That sounds intense."

"It can be," he agreed. "I contributed to the problem, so they sent me here one summer and I loved it. I got my act together, then come spring, I had a full-on regression, until my mom told me I could come here for the summer even if it wasn't as a punishment."

"What did you do?"

"Loads of things. Muck out the stables, repair the fences, lift heavy things, clean Mr. Embry's pool…"

"Sounds like the ideal summer," I teased.

"You're missing the part where as soon as my chores were done, I got to ride the horses and swim in said pool and…"

"Jump the fences?"

"We tried, but my horse didn't have it in him. I was too afraid to try it again with a different one."

"Sounds traumatic."

"It was," he agreed. "But I didn't let it stop me."

"I always wanted to go riding." There were stables on our property, but I don't know the last time they held horses.

"I can take you some time, if you want," he offered.

"That would be amazing!"

"Lucy!" Embry called over before I could thank Eric. Gabriel and Embry were already standing and ready to go, with neither of them looking happy.

"I'll see you around." Sam was a hugger, so I didn't think anything of it when Eric took me in his arms to say goodbye.

"Come by anytime, Lucy," Charlie told me with a hug as well.

"WHAT'S WRONG?" I asked as we walked to the villa.

"Nothing," Embry assured me in a way that told me that was not the case.

"Are we leaving again?"

"No, we're going to stay here a while." I was surprised it was Gabriel who endorsed it.

"Get some sleep, *Tesoro*, there'll be lots to do in the morning." Embry kissed the top of my head once we got inside the villa, both of them setting off to their own rooms. I went up to the spare bedroom I'd changed in and wondered what they had in store for me.

CHAPTER SIX

*H*enry had clearly stuck to his promise, as he was there beside me, walking through the countryside, making Annabelle laugh. She felt a familiarity towards him that told me he hadn't only called on her once, but many times. Still, it wasn't the all-encompassing, can't eat, can't sleep, can't breathe without him love she had once had with Gabriel, nor was it the surprising but steady love she had found with Embry. Being with Henry was doing little to make her forget the men she had loved before, and still did, judging by the thoughts swimming around in her head. At the same time, Henry was someone she could see herself caring about. Especially if Gabriel was no longer an option.*

The more we walked, the more I got the feeling this was Henry's property rather than a countryside. He had lovely gardens, just like Annabelle's father's, that you could walk in for hours. I saw lots of exotic flowers, as well as the most gorgeous roses. Some of the plants did not have much going for them appearance-wise, but they smelt heavenly. Every once in a while, Henry would stop so we could smell them, or regale her with all of the cooking uses and healing properties of a particular plant.

"I've never seen eyes like yours before," Annabelle said after a few

minutes in silence, with him smiling down at her. It didn't make her uncomfortable per se, but it scared her, because it was the way Gabriel had often looked at her.

"Is that a good thing, or a bad thing?" Henry inquired, looking into her eyes. They caught Annabelle off guard because she wasn't used to it; how very dark they were. It was like the iris surrounding the pupil had simply absorbed its color, so the entire middle part of the eye was black. I spent the past fifteen years watching Embry and Gabriel's eyes go darker and darker, so it was the knowledge that Henry was Gifted that shocked me more than the color.

"I'm not sure yet." She looked closer, trying to figure it out. The darkness didn't scare her, but it wasn't welcoming either.

Henry sighed before telling her a story. "It was an accident. Years ago, I was playing with my nephew and ran into a woman who was carrying a pot of some chemical that got into my eye and turned it black." I wondered how much of it was true and how much he came up with to answer such questions.

"That's terrible," Annabelle said, wondering what kind of chemical could change the color of one's eyes. Both eyes. "Can you still see everything?"

"It was a long recovery. Eventually everything healed, although the black remained."

"They say that eyes are the windows to the soul." I don't know why she said it, but the idea seemed to intrigue him.

"And what do you see in mine?" He said it low, like a whisper, only there was something excitingly dangerous in it.

She looked carefully before admitting, "All I see is myself." She laughed, but he looked happy with her answer.

"And I pray that is how it always will be."

I woke up from another memory dream and couldn't get back to sleep. It was earlier than the teenager in me on summer vacation wanted to, but it was hopefully early enough that I could talk to Embry about the memory I saw yesterday.

HE WAS ALONE at the kitchen table, sipping an espresso. There were two slices of toast with peanut butter and sliced bananas at the spot beside him. But Embry hated bananas.

"I heard you getting dressed," he told my confused look.

"You knew I was coming?" I sat down and took a bite, savoring my toast with a welcome hint of cinnamon.

"I wondered what you would see once we got here. It's one of the main reasons I chose it, but I knew you would eventually see other things as well."

"I don't only see the memories," I reminded him.

"Hence the apology breakfast," he told me, getting a smile. I could tell he was hesitating to ask, possibly not wanting to scar me any further, but he also wanted to know.

"It was your anniversary," I shared, making his eyes go wide.

"Which one?"

Part of me wanted to know what elaborate plans he put into action over the years, but I did not want to live through them, so I didn't ask.

"Fifth." I picked up the second toast.

For a moment he was lost in the memory, then he smiled. "Helen had a nightmare and slept in the bed with us." He got up to make himself another espresso, relieved.

"Which is the only reason I can still sit here beside you and look you in the eyes."

"How is it when it happens? Do you hear their thoughts and know all their secrets, or…"

"It's weird," I tried to find a way to explain it. "I don't have access to all their thoughts and memories, just from those moments. I'm still me, but I see what they're seeing, and feel what they feel…"

"I'm sorry…"

"That too, but I meant emotions. Like I didn't know who she was waiting for in the closet, but I knew she was excited to see them more than annoyed that they were taking so long, and that whoever it was, she loved them. With all her heart. I haven't seen any of my ancestors that happy yet."

"Thank you," he said like it meant a lot, but I don't think he needed me to tell him how she felt. I looked at him expectantly, but he was satisfied with the conversation and ready to move on. "What?" he asked when I looked at him with a mix of guilt and curiosity.

"I didn't see you naked, but I still have a million questions."

He nearly choked on his coffee before looking at me with a huge smile.

"I forgot about that part."

"The part where you never told me you were married to Beth?" I put it plainly.

"Keep it down," he warned.

I looked at him with confusion before I realized, "Gabriel doesn't know?"

"He might suspect there was something. He knows we were close, but no, he does not know the full extent of our relationship."

"Five years," I pointed out.

"When Beth's husband died, we both came to David's funeral. Gabriel stayed a couple of weeks, but it was his turn to be the guardian of the new safe house. I offered to stay and help her get things settled, and…we fell in love. When Gabriel came back to check on her, I was still there, so he stayed away."

"You guys are ridiculous. Do you even know why you're fighting?"

"Time heals things when you move on, not when you spend your life being reminded of it and waiting for her to come back." There was a sadness to him as he said it, but he wasn't talking about himself.

I could tell he didn't want me to push, so I moved on to the big question I was holding back, ever since I saw the memory of Beth discovering the Prophecy. "I saw something else a while ago that I didn't know how to bring up, but…"

"What is it?" he reassured me that I could ask him anything, but I knew my question would break his heart, whether it was his baby or not.

"In the memory that made me fall out of the tree, Beth—"

"Did you tell her?" Gabriel walked into the kitchen and silenced me. My heart stopped, wondering how much he heard.

"Tell me what?" I asked once I realized he was talking to Embry about something completely unrelated. Embry looked guilty instead of relieved, as I would have expected.

"We discussed it, and since you don't want to be left behind, we're going to train you," Gabriel shared.

"Really?" I perked up and finished my toast.

"Don't get too excited," Embry warned.

"I don't know what happened in the washroom," I caught on.

"Annabelle could do magic," Gabriel admitted, looking at me with guilt in his eyes.

"She was a witch?" I tried to remember exactly what he told me at the plantation. "You said she was burnt at the stake, but she was innocent."

"Of the crimes they were accusing her of. Not necessarily of witchcraft." He used a technicality, but it was still a lie. "The night before she died, she did a spell to track the men who were after her, to see how close they were to finding us."

"And…" I wondered if she fought them with her supposed powers, but Embry was looking at Gabriel as expectantly as I was.

"They were close, so she turned herself in," Gabriel said like that was the end of it.

"One spell doesn't mean anything," I decided. "Have any of the Bearers since Annabelle demonstrated any kind of magical ability?"

"No one has tried." Gabriel gave me a look. He wasn't mentioning it, but we both knew that what happened in the washroom either meant I was Gifted, or a witch. Since I didn't die, the obvious answer was that I take after Annabelle in the magic department.

"I don't want to try either," I turned them down. "Why don't you teach me how to fight with weapons, and then we can see how it goes?" I suggested.

"You feel more comfortable getting close to people with weapons?" Embry asked, surprised.

"I can control the weapons." I couldn't say as much for my hands.

"You can learn to control the magic too." Embry put his hand on mine, showing me he didn't fear them like I did. "We're no match for the people that are hunting you, but if you can control your powers, you might be."

I did want to learn to fight back against Donovan and his master, to make sure they couldn't hurt anyone else the way they hurt Sam, but I couldn't imagine I would be a match for them.

"Are you going to teach me?" I raised my eyebrows at Embry.

"I can show you how Annabelle did her tracking spell, but we don't have that kind of magic." Gabriel handed me a book he'd brought from upstairs. "But that is why we have her Shadow Book."

"Book of Shadows," Embry corrected, but I focused on Gabriel.

"If you're uncomfortable, we can stop, but there has to be a reason you have this, and wouldn't you rather be able to control it next time?" He kept his eyes locked on mine in earnest, until I had to look away.

"Okay," I reluctantly agreed. I never wanted my hands to betray me like that again. It would also be nice to get ahead of the bad guys for once. To actually stand a chance at defeating them without losing even more people.

"We can go out into the yard and try some easy, simple spells. Work our way up, okay?" Gabriel offered.

"Okay," I repeated, following him when he got up and headed for the patio doors. "You're not coming?" I asked Embry when he stayed back, bringing our dirty plates to the sink.

"He has even less experience with it than I do," Gabriel assured me with an encouraging smile, but nothing about that statement made me feel better.

"I'll be around." Embry nodded for me to go.

"WHAT EXACTLY AM I DOING?" I asked Gabriel when we got to a blanket on the grass. It was like a picnic, only there were maps, crystals, and a book instead of food and wine.

"I saw her doing a tracking spell, so I figured we could start with that." He sat down cross-legged and took out a map.

"Who am I looking for?" I asked.

"We could look for Donovan to make sure he isn't anywhere near us," he suggested.

"Would that mean he could track me?" I was not a fan of that scenario.

"According to Annabelle, there's map tracking and essence tracking. As long as we only do map tracking, you'll be fine."

"Couldn't Donovan trick a tracking spell? With a cloaking spell?" I asked.

"Is that something you read in the books? Or saw on TV?" He was amused by my question.

"There's no magic in the Chronicles, and I haven't read the Book of Shadows," I gave him the answer. "Even if it was on TV, it still makes sense."

"I'm sure you can, but I doubt they would be using one. We have never hunted them back, or posed any kind of threat," he pointed out.

"You think this will work?" I asked, eying the candles he lit and placed around a map of the world. "Even if I have no skills whatsoever?"

"The way Annabelle explained it, magic wasn't a skill she had to practice or cultivate to use. If you had it in you and did the right thing, or said the right words, something would happen." As he spoke, he took a piece of paper and started drawing on it with a pencil, fast strokes with a sure hand. It wasn't until he handed it to me that I saw it was of Donovan, accurate enough to give me chills.

"Don't get your hopes up," I warned, following the book's instructions by tying a string around one of the crystals and holding it in my right hand. The roughly drawn sketch of Donovan's face was on my left palm. "Inveniet Donovan."

I closed my eyes and repeated the words, picturing him in my head and feeling the hairs on the back of my neck tense up. I felt like an absolute idiot and was terrified of what I might find out.

"It's okay, relax your mind and think of Donovan," Gabriel encouraged. He sounded supportive, not at all upset it wasn't working, but I did not have his confidence.

I tried to clear my mind, but every time I pictured Donovan, I either saw him giving the order for his man to slit Sam's throat, or threatening to cut off every one of Clara's freckles… one time I saw Donovan, surrounded by darkness, but he had such an ominous look that I completely shut down and needed to start all over again.

After at least a half an hour of trying with no success, Gabriel decided we should attempt a different spell, and flipped to one of the first pages in the book. The entire spread was covered in writing on how to make objects float.

"Can I have a water break?" I asked, feeling overwhelmed. I wasn't used to being bad at learning things, or to accepting magic as a real thing.

"I'll go get you a glass. Try and relax. Don't put so much pressure on yourself." He gave me an encouraging smile before going to the house.

"How's it going?" Embry came over from the stables, where he'd been watching us from for the last fifteen minutes.

"Terrible. I think we made a mistake, and it wasn't actually me who made her disappear."

"Or it came to you when you needed it, but you haven't figured out how to get it when you want it," he argued. "Unless you don't want it?"

"No, I love turning someone's grandmother into a pile of ash during their Sunday brunch." I hid behind sarcasm. He raised an eyebrow when I said grandmother, but otherwise saw right through me.

"I know it's scary. Beth told me she was terrified the first time it happened to her," he shared, expecting my shocked reaction.

"Did she ever figure it out?" It made sense that free-spirited Beth, who wrote of superstitions and lived in New Orleans, would have inherited the magic as well.

"Of course. You will too." He nodded to reassure me.

"What did she do?"

"Lots of research." He gave me a smile. "Once she was making things happen rather than having things happen to her, it was a lot less scary."

"This isn't something I can read a book to solve," I argued with his logic.

"Maybe not any book, but the Book of Shadows can definitely help. It will teach you spells that you can master, to help you control your magic instead of it controlling you."

"Mind over matter?" I brought my hand to my head, applying pressure to relieve the beginning of a headache.

"Or practice makes perfect."

"I'm trying to practice, but nothing's happening."

"It helps if you're not convincing yourself you can't do it."

"I'm not convincing myself; my incapability is convincing me," I argued. He raised an eyebrow at me and waited. "I also don't want to find him. When I think of him...all I feel is fear, and then I think of Sam, and I have to get out of there."

"Maybe you should try finding someone you actually want to find," he suggested. "And believe you can do it. I do."

"Gabriel is taking over because Annabelle kept her powers from you, and he saw her do one spell...but I feel like you're sitting on a lot more experience." I eyed him expectantly.

"We didn't have secrets from each other. And she didn't just dabble when she was in trouble. It was a way of life in the Quarter."

"She was a full-blown witch?"

"She helped people," he didn't label it.

"About the other memory..."

"It's okay," he assured me, as I struggled over not wanting to hurt him, but needing to know.

"Beth was pregnant," I shared. "I thought it was with Helen, but she was there too."

"Our son, Jackson." He gave me a smile, but his eyes were focused on a memory from the past, not on me.

I had a million more questions, but Gabriel came back, so Embry retreated to the stables.

"Ready?" Gabriel handed me the water.

"I want to try the tracking spell one more time first," I told him, taking a sip.

"Of course." He set everything up for me.

Instead of Donovan, I pictured Clara laughing and smiling, running around the orchard. I said the words to myself, with my heart yearning to see her, take her in my arms, and protect her from all the bad things I brought into her life. My hand that wasn't holding the string rubbed the plastic ring she gave me for my last birthday.

All of a sudden, the string tensed so the crystal was no longer dangling, but pointing at a specific location. I looked up from the map, that showed Cape Cod, and saw the horror in Gabriel's eyes.

"I have people there, but I'll send word…" I could see him struggling to find a way to protect them without putting me at risk, and realized I should have filled him in on my plans beforehand.

"It's okay." I put my hand on his. "Part of my problem is that I don't want to see Donovan, so I looked for Clara."

"Clara's the one on the east coast, at the Beach House?" He verified.

"Looks like." I couldn't help but smile that it worked.

"Not Donovan." He relaxed a little.

"I don't know where he is, but hopefully not."

"That's really smart." He beamed at me.

"I had help." He followed my gaze and saw Embry looking over at us.

"He does get you," Gabriel said.

"I think he might also get this stuff more than you give him credit for." I was hoping that somewhere along the way, the two of them would be able to put their differences, or similarities, aside and forgive each other.

"That's often the case." He surprised me. "Don't get excited," he warned, noticing the smile that was spreading on my face before I understood he was just stating a fact.

"Unbelievable." I shook my head.

"A three-hundred-year-old habit is hard to break," he defended himself.

"Are you even trying?" I brought my palm to my forehead and ran my fingers back through my hair, sighing out my frustration.

"I'm here, aren't I?"

"Because you have to be."

"You should have seen us with Rosie." A shadow passed his face, but was gone as fast as it came. "And Cassie, before she sat us down and gave us a severe talking to." He smiled at the memory.

"But it didn't change anything?"

"We have been incredibly civil ever since," he assured me.

"Maybe try nice and friendly from now on. See how that goes?"

"I can try," he said with a shrug.

"He's pretty awesome." I looked over to Embry, who was now sitting on a bushel of hay with Charlie, both of them laughing.

"I remember," Gabriel said with a smile, but I could see a hint of sadness over what he lost.

I rolled my eyes before we worked some more on my tracking spells. We went through all the people I wanted to see, finding them exactly where they were supposed to be, before I finally tried Donovan again. I still didn't want to see him, but at least I knew it would work if I put myself through the fear.

I kept my eyes closed, even after the crystal moved.

"California." Gabriel checked the map.

"Then he isn't coming after us." I breathed a sigh of relief.

"Not yet," he said with an edge. It was only a matter of time.

CHAPTER SEVEN

Working on spells left me exhausted by the time I got to bed every night, but at least I felt like I was accomplishing things. I couldn't spend my days reading the Chronicles anymore, so I tried to wake up early and read a few pages over breakfast.

"Anything interesting?" Embry asked, walking into the kitchen. He put a cup under the Nespresso machine for his morning shot of caffeine. He looked more at home here than anywhere else, even if he said he hadn't been back in years.

"Haven't you read them before?"

"I have, but you and I have very different interests. I could spend hours poring over a handwritten grocery list from Beth, which would bore you to tears."

"Fair enough." I considered his question. "We all have different handwriting. Even though we're identical replicas or whatever. Like this note was slipped in Beth's section, but it was clearly written by Cassie."

"Clearly," he agreed with me, but I got the impression he had no idea. "I could tell it wasn't Beth," he admitted.

"And Beth decides out of nowhere to leave blank pages, or

ones that have nothing but pictures of teddy bears and imaginary flowers."

"You sound upset by this." He smiled, the pictures making him a lot happier than they made me.

"Cassie and Beth had the most interesting sections, full of adventures, remedies, and potentially useful information. I thought I had pages and pages to get through, but out of her last twenty, ten of them are blank," I explained.

"You were gypped."

"Exactly."

"I can't defend her ways, although that is a beautiful work of art that deserves to be admired," he said of the six-legged horse we landed on. "I might have something to make up for it, for you at least."

"A museum?" I teased.

"An apothecary."

"Isn't that a pharmacy?"

"It's time you meet Ingrid." He finished his espresso and went upstairs.

By the time I came down after getting dressed and ready for a potential adventure, Embry and Gabriel were both at the bottom of the stairs.

"Family outing?" I asked.

"If you're leaving the property, we're both coming," Gabriel explained, giving Embry a warning look.

"Are we going far?" Excitement mixed with fear to form a ball in my stomach. Adventures were exciting when I thought protecting me was a ridiculous precaution, but I was coming to enjoy the protective cocoons that made me feel slightly safer than the world at large.

"Just the Quarter," Embry said like it was nothing at all, so I pretended to know exactly where that was. Gabriel, for his part, was ever-alert, as if we were heading right into a war zone.

WE DROVE to a parking lot where they gave me a sunhat to keep me slightly disguised, with my long hair falling down my back to cover the birthmark. Embry walked ahead of us on the pedestrian street to show the way, while Gabriel stayed back with me. The Big Bad wasn't currently on our tail, but he was going to be looking for the three of us together, and we didn't want to make things too easy for him.

"Have you been here before?" I asked Gabriel. We were keeping a leisurely pace to not draw suspicion. I was grateful that I didn't have to half-run to keep up, but I could tell he wished we were going a lot faster.

"New Orleans and the Quarter, many times, but never to the apothecary."

"You stayed with Embry when you came?" I found it weird that Eric met him, since the guys avoided each other if it wasn't to protect me.

"I've met Charlie loads of times over the years. I met Eric once when he was very little. Charlie asked for Embry's help when he was away somewhere, so he sent me."

"What kind of help?"

"Neighborly stuff." He shrugged it off, which could mean they didn't want me to know, or he didn't want to make a big deal of whatever he did.

"Where do you go when you're not with me?" I asked. "Before this summer, when you weren't visiting me at the manor, where did you live?"

"Why do you ask?" He looked to me with a slightly raised eyebrow.

"I've been realizing how little I knew about you and Embry before this. How much I still don't know."

"You weren't supposed to know," he said simply, but part of me was hurt.

"Not even where you live or what you do? I can't believe I never asked."

"If we had shown up when you were older you would have asked all the questions, but you were so young when we met you. By the time you cared about those things, we were no longer new, or strangers, we were just there."

"I was also afraid of you," I admitted.

"Of me?" He sounded surprised, so I looked at his face to see if he was joking. It was as dark and intense as ever.

"Sometimes there were glimpses of what I assume is the you from your first life, but most of the time you were this stoic presence that kept his distance and dressed entirely in black."

"What changed?" he asked me with a smile, since I'd described what he was like to this day.

"I saw the glimpses," I admitted, nervous under the very different intensity of his current gaze.

"Of what?" he pressed.

"Of someone who cared." I shrugged. "Mostly about Annabelle, but sometimes about me too."

"Only sometimes?" Gabriel asked.

I could feel my face blushing, before Embry came out of an alley I hadn't even seen him turn into.

"Over here," Embry ushered us to follow.

"I.V. Strauss Apothecary?" I read the sign. It was old and musty, like it hadn't been changed in centuries, but the window dressings made it look like the inside was a Pottery Barn.

"I think you'll enjoy it." Embry had the same look on his face as when he gave one of his thoughtful presents and waited impatiently for you to discover the magic inside.

Wind chimes went off when I opened the door, but they were coming from somewhere deeper inside the store. The first fifteen feet were exactly like an Anthropologie or some fancy home decor and knickknack store. Different sized jars lined the walls, fauteuils were covered with soft throws, antique tables housed assortments of crystals...there were minimal items on the shelves and lots of open spaces. It had way more of a one-of-a-kind vibe than most stores this size.

The next few aisles were covered in pots, jars, bags of ingredients, and spices. It smelled like a combination of cinnamon, vanilla, and pepper, with a vintage register at the end.

The rest of the store was separated by burgundy curtains that looked like a wall until you got close enough to see the sheer section that served as a doorway.

"Ing?" Embry called once we were the only patrons.

"Em?" A voice came from behind the curtains a second before they parted to a cloud of smoke. A little girl rushed to us and nearly jumped into Embry's arms. She was wearing a burgundy dress with an olive-colored shawl, her long blonde hair cascading down her back.

I raised an eyebrow before she looked around and saw they weren't alone.

"Oh...I didn't know you brought company, I would have kept..." She was incredibly nervous, with her eyes darting to the curtains like she wanted to run back inside.

"They're friends," Embry assured her.

"Beth!" she exclaimed when she spotted me. She came close and took my hands in hers. "Is this Marilyn's daughter?"

"Lucy," Embry agreed.

"He warned me, of course, but you look just like her," she told me.

"Except for the hair," Embry pointed out.

"No, you're what? Eighteen? Nineteen?" Ingrid asked, getting a good look at me.

"Eighteen," I said.

"She kept it like this until her twenties. I told her she shouldn't cut her beautiful hair, that no man would ever look at her…" She looked from Embry to Gabriel and changed her mind on what came next. "But she looked gorgeous with the bob as well."

"You're the Ingrid who was like a sister to her?" I'd seen the name in the Chronicles many times recently.

"They were inseparable," Gabriel agreed, letting me know that although he hadn't been to the apothecary, he still knew Ingrid, or at least of her.

"We were the same age, once upon a time," Ingrid told me. "The day she moved here, I decided we would be best friends. We stayed that way until the day…until the end."

"I'm sorry," I said of her loss, before the wind chimes went off somewhere above us.

"I'll be right back." I could tell it was Ingrid, but she now looked to be about thirty.

"What happened?" I asked Embry.

"I tricked her into showing you her true self, but she normally presents herself as older, so people don't assume they can take advantage of her, and child services don't get involved."

"Is that her Gift, or…"

"A spell?" Embry finished for me. "I believe she was a witch in her first life, but her Gift is to alter your perception of reality. I would not want to get on her bad side."

"She looks so young…"

"Eight," Gabriel shared. "They were both thirteen when I first met them, but Beth had been living here since she was four." Which meant Beth was there for Ingrid's death, and coming back to life, before she found out about Gifted and what she was. Unless Ingrid kept it from her, but I didn't think that was the case.

"Where were we?" Ingrid came back to us and waited until the customers left the shop before becoming a woman roughly my age.

"I brought Lucy here to see if you had anything useful to

teach her, or wisdom to impart, as she follows in Beth's footsteps."

"I could feel it the moment you walked in," she told me.

"Feel what?" I asked before the chimes rang out again, a warning for her to assume a different appearance.

"Mr. Fraser, how can I help you?" the thirty-year-old version of Ingrid asked a man in his fifties who slowly made his way to the register, shaking his head.

"They got Frankie too." He sat in the antique chair like it was too hard for him to stand with the weight of his news.

"Who got him?" Embry asked.

"Who are they?" Was Mr. Fraser's response.

"Friends," Ingrid assured him, but he looked at us with suspicion, before I felt like a huge hand was trying to push its way into my skull. I aggressively shook my head and grabbed my temple, making Embry and Gabriel turn to me before Mr. Fraser cried out, "Ow!" and they all turned to him.

"I said they were friends!" Ingrid got upset and slapped the back of his head, which made him cry out again.

"What did he do to you?" Gabriel came to stand between us with a look that could kill.

"I don't know." I looked to Ingrid.

"Mr. Fraser can read minds. Usually, he's in and out with none the wiser, but I've seen that happen once before." Ingrid was smiling, which told me the last time she saw it was with Beth.

"Is everyone in New Orleans Gifted?" I asked.

"He's not Gifted, he just pays a heavy price to age very slowly." She put a green ceramic pot on the counter for him.

"You trade in secrets that you steal," Gabriel accused, the vein in his forehead pulsing.

"She's a friend." Embry stood between Gabriel and Ingrid.

"Who got Frankie?" I brought us back to before everyone was defensive and on edge.

"We don't know," Mr. Fraser admitted, looking like he trusted me even less now that I blocked him out. Or maybe he could see that I looked like Beth.

"Frankie is the fourth person to disappear in the middle of the night. There's no sign of forced entry, no struggle, nothing to make the cops take any of it seriously."

"Did they maybe just run away?" I ventured.

"One of them was a six-year-old boy. He didn't run away." Mr. Fraser was upset.

"He was kidnapped?" My heart tightened with thoughts of Clara. "Cops would investigate that."

"They think his father took him, so they put out an Amber Alert, but they're looking for the father, not the child."

"Isn't that the most likely scenario?"

"Not when the father was a violent SOB who is buried in the backyard," Mr. Fraser said under his breath.

"He read it off the mother, he didn't participate," Ingrid assured us.

"Was everyone who disappeared a patron?" Embry asked with concern, putting his hand protectively on Ingrid's arm.

"No, just Frankie and Billy's mother," Ingrid defended herself. "We see the missing posters all around town."

"Do you think it's—" I started to ask the guys, but Embry and Gabriel both shook their heads, even though missing Gifted was one of their signs for danger being close by.

Mr. Fraser didn't look like he would be leaving any time soon, so Embry and Gabriel exchanged a look.

"We have to head out, but we'll try to stop by another time," Embry told Ingrid.

"Bring her by on Wednesday. It's usually quiet, so I can show her a few things," she said before grabbing the middle book in a stack she was using as a table for a vintage Tiffany lamp. "In the meantime, a little light reading." She smiled as she handed me the large volume and brought Mr. Fraser behind the curtain.

. . .

ON THE WAY BACK, Embry walked with me, and Gabriel went off on his own.

"What's up?" he asked me.

"How much do you trust her?"

"Beth made her godmother to Helen, and to Jack," he said simply.

My mom chose Mr. and Mrs. Boyd for me, because she didn't have anyone else she trusted, and you couldn't be baptized without godparents. I considered this a moment, then asked, "Did you ever think of Gabriel for godfather?"

"He was my first choice." He gave me a sad smile. "Why don't you trust Ingrid?"

"She's basically paying a man to invade people's minds and tell her their secrets," I pointed out.

"He's an unsavory character, but he's harmless. And it's more like she pays him not to tell anyone else what he finds out when he hears people's thoughts," he defended her.

"He was pushing hard to get into mine." I could still feel a pressure, although that might be the wall my mind put up to keep him out.

"If every door you came across flew open when you walked up, wouldn't you try a few things if you suddenly found one that was closed?"

CHAPTER EIGHT

My next lesson was making things float, which evolved into seeing how much I could move before I lost all accuracy and safety went out the window. I got nervous when floating heavier or dangerous things over people, or anything involving breakable objects, which usually made me lose concentration and drop them. I managed to lift a really big rock, but a mole ran out from under it, so I panicked and dropped it. Thank God it wasn't on the mole

"How is this useful?" I asked, rubbing my hands together to stop the tingling.

"Patience, padawan," Embry teased.

"What's next, Master Yoda?"

"I appreciate the enthusiasm, but I think that's enough for today."

"We have things to take care of, but Charlie will be next door if you need anything." Gabriel sounded reluctant, but looked resigned.

"Is this the kind of thing where you leave me for days?" It wasn't that I hadn't enjoyed spending time with Terrence and learning to knit when they abandoned me last time, but I didn't want to be left behind again.

"We're looking into the disappearances, making sure they don't have anything to do with you," Embry assured me.

"But you'll be back today?" I verified.

"Take the rest of the day off and we'll be back in time for dinner."

I looked into Embry's eyes and decided I trusted them to come back to me.

"Just don't leave the property," Gabriel amended.

"And let us know where you are at all times."

I rolled my eyes at their predictability before going to my room to get the Chronicles. I probably would have secretly explored the house, looking for clues on Helen, Jack, and Beth, but I would never snoop when there was a possibility Embry could find me.

I brought the huge book to a garden swing deep in the yard and got comfy. I was half-hoping and half-terrified that Beth would use the Chronicles as a diary, but she only wrote about noteworthy adventures, remedies, potions, and some spells. So far there was absolutely no mention of Embry as more than her protector. Helen was the only child in evidence, from drawings and scribbles rather than actual mentions.

I was reading about a celebration Beth did with her friend Ingrid, when Charlie walked up to me.

"I'm sorry, there isn't usually anyone here when I take my afternoon stroll," he apologized.

"I can go if you…"

"No, I was rejoicing at the company," he corrected, taking a seat beside me on the swing.

"Company would be nice," I agreed.

"Isn't school out for the summer?" He nodded to the Chronicles.

"Stories from my ancestors." I closed the volume, not sure I wanted him to know about any spells or magic it might mention.

"Don't stop on my account. I spent sixty years with a woman who always had a book in her hands," he said fondly. "She died last spring, but there wasn't a single idea that she shared with the world before sharing it with me first." He must have noticed my reaction, wondering why he was such a controlling and restrictive husband, because he elaborated, "She wrote books, and I always got to read them first."

"What kind of books?"

"Mostly on science, but she wanted them to be understood by the masses. People like me, not just the ones with PhDs. That's not to say I'm not smart, but it's a different kind of smart than she was."

"You're Mr. Haynes," I realized, remembering when Embry told me about Laurel Haynes, whose husband was Gifted because he was the one who convinced her to publish her books. She would have written them no matter what, but shared them on a much smaller scale if he wasn't around.

"No, Laurel kept her maiden name for the books, that way no one bothered us out here. It's Mr. Finch, but friends call me Charlie." His hand was callused from a lifetime working outdoors, but when I shook it, I was surprised to find it was still soft.

"Did my grandmother know her too?"

"Your grandfather introduced us." He smiled at my surprise.

"I never met him," I admitted.

"Of course, you didn't. But I think you would have gotten along wonderfully."

"All I know about him is that he liked vintage cars and died when my mom was in high school."

"That's a shame." He looked genuinely hurt over it.

"Grams died when I was really young too." I have memories of my Grams where she is kind and loving, but also a bit paranoid and removed from the outside world. Mr. and Mrs. Boyd would tell me she was different once, but the only example they had was that she used to have parties and visitors and go out all the time before my grandfather died. "You could tell me about them, if you're not too busy some time."

"I would love to." He beamed. "I have a million stories. I wouldn't know where to start."

"At the beginning?" I suggested.

"The beginning of her? Or of us?"

"When did you first meet her?"

"I can't remember not knowing her." He tried to think. "Her mom brought her here every summer, even after they moved to Boston. I met her before I could walk or talk or any of that."

"Did you two ever..." There was something about the way he said it that made me wonder if they were more than just childhood friends.

"First love and first kiss," he agreed. "I still get nervous around Embry sometimes."

"He was overprotective?" I smiled.

"Very," he agreed. "It was a weird dynamic if you didn't know what was going on."

"Probably weirder if you did," I pointed out.

"Arguably, yes."

"Who broke who's heart?"

"It wasn't like that," he brushed it off. "She was amazing. This fierce girl from the North who didn't let anyone tell her what to do. It was usually just the two of us, but anyone who met her fell for her. I was lucky enough to be her favorite person in Louisiana," he said, which sounded exactly like what I was asking.

"When did you meet my grandfather?"

"The summer we turned sixteen, we drove to Nashville to see Johnny Cash at the Grand Ole Opry. I won't lie and pretend I wasn't hoping something would happen, but Grant came over to say hi to her, and the way she looked at him, I knew she would never be mine."

"*She* broke *your* heart," I concluded.

"She would have," he agreed. "But by the time she admitted to liking him as much as I knew she did, Grant had spent quite a few weekends in New Orleans, most of them with his best friend, Laurel."

"Were they like you and my Grams?"

"I am told it was like kissing her brother, so she was relieved when he told her about the girl he met at a concert, and she orchestrated most of their trips."

"For him to see Grams, or so she could see you?" I called him on it.

"Her motives grew more selfish as the summer went on." He smiled.

"Did Grams still spend every summer here after she got married?"

"Once she went to college, she had to go home to Boston in the summers, but we were all at Louisiana State together, so I still got to see her."

"What did they study?" I had no idea what Grams did other than be rich and take care of me.

"Grant was in the science department with Laurel. Astrophysics and space stuff." He shrugged like it was all Chinese to him. "And your Grams was the only lawyer I have ever trusted. She refused to take on clients who were guilty and deserved to pay for their crimes."

"I don't think you're allowed to do that," I argued.

"Not technically, but she did."

He went on to tell me about her entire process once she had her practice set up, where she would interview potential clients.

"If the crime was one she found reprehensible and they were guilty, she sent them away. If it was a crime she might have committed if she were in their shoes, she would defend the innocent and the guilty alike."

"A lawyer with a moral code." I shook my head. It was hard to picture Grams as a powerful lawyer.

"And how many times did she get you out of something?" Eric came over, wearing dark blue jeans and a green plaid shirt with a cowboy hat, which would have made me laugh my head off, only it somehow worked for him.

"Only the things she got me into."

"I'm sensing a story." I smiled, hoping Charlie would share.

"Lots of them, but I believe my grandson came over for a reason."

"I'm down for stories," Eric assured his grandfather. "But if Lucy would like to accompany me, I was going to go riding."

"We've got time to finish this later," Charlie told me.

"Then I would love to go horseback riding with you. I'll change and be right back," I told Eric before heading inside to put the Chronicles away and change into a pair of pants.

WHEN I GOT to the stables, Eric had a beautiful, butterscotch colored horse saddled and waiting for me.

"This is Donner," he introduced.

"And who is this?" I asked of the chestnut mare he had for himself.

"Rudolf." He looked embarrassed. "We were very young when we chose their names, and it was December, so..."

"Reindeer," I let him know I understood. "Do you guys get snow here?"

"No, we don't. My oldest sister convinced us that horses were reindeer who lived in warmer climates."

"I'm sensing a lot of these tricks."

"My entire childhood," he agreed. "But now they're having kids and I'm their older and wiser uncle, so I'm making up for it."

"I didn't know you were the vengeful type," I remarked.

"It's not revenge so much as my duty," he argued.

"You're close?"

"Not like when we were all living together, but they come out here every summer, we get together at Christmas... I try to make it to all the birthday parties, but there are lots."

"How many nieces and nephews do you have?"

"Eighteen and a half."

"Missing body parts, or someone's still pregnant?" I got him to laugh.

"Franny married a guy who already had a four-year-old daughter, so she calls herself my half. As far as I'm concerned, it's nineteen, but the nickname makes her happy."

"My niece likes to introduce me as her sister-aunt to kids at school."

"But she's really your niece?" he asked.

"I was orphaned when I was four and the couple that took me in had a son. We grew up together, so I feel like his daughter is my niece, but I also still live with them." I tried to find a less tragic way to explain that every member of my family died, so I won't ever have a sister or a niece, technically speaking. He also didn't need to know that I'd lost Sam too. Maybe I was cursed.

"Sister-aunt," he agreed with Clara's title for me.

"I guess so." I rolled my eyes.

ERIC TOOK us through a path in the wooded area, toward the swamplands.

"Not a fan?" he asked when I kept slapping myself to kill the bugs.

"It's beautiful, but I'm being eaten alive."

"Zombies or cannibals?" he asked.

"Mosquitoes. They're not bothering you?"

"Guess your blood is sweeter." He smiled. "This was my favorite place to play as a kid, until grandpa freaked out."

"Is it dangerous?"

"The mosquitoes carry a deadly virus," he teased. "I think people might drown in the swamps sometimes, or there's alligators, but it had more to do with me bringing half the swamp back to the house with me."

"That could be upsetting."

"Now the horses play in the mud, and I can outrun the bugs."

"I doubt that," I argued as he started slapping himself as well.

"Come on." He brought me around the property, which was beautiful, but also very different from our land in Boston.

He told me more about his family and his childhood with Charlie while I shared stories about life with Sam and Deanna, as if this was just a summer trip and everything would be back to normal once I went home.

WHEN WE BROUGHT the horses back to the stables, he showed me how to take the saddle off and let me brush Donner.

"Out of all the reindeer, why Donner?" I asked as I brushed. "I get Rudolph, but Comet, Cupid, Blitzen, Dasher, Dancer, Prancer, Vixen…"

"He came seventh." Eric shrugged.

"You're the youngest?" I guessed.

"They would never say unwanted, but my siblings were all born very close together, and I came as an afterthought."

"Maybe they missed having a baby."

"I'm Charlie's favorite now, so that's good enough for me."

"You liked it here because you got to be an only child."

"And there is nothing wrong with that." he laughed at being caught.

"Nothing at all," I assured him. I had wished for siblings, in the sense that I wished my parents had been around long enough to have more kids, but I was perfectly happy when I had Sam.

"Same time tomorrow?" Eric asked me.

"I have no idea what they have planned."

"Are you their prisoner?" He was mostly teasing, but I could tell he was curious.

"I thought you knew them?"

"Embry comes sometimes, but it's more like I know his house really well."

"I have yet to explore it."

"Most of the fun stuff is behind locked doors."

"It usually is," I agreed.

"Not a prisoner?" he verified.

"It depends on your definition." I considered it, but he looked concerned, so I backtracked. "They're looking out for me. I'm ninety-nine percent sure they're the good guys."

"Well, with that glowing recommendation..." He laughed, and I did too, until we ran into Gabriel. Literally, because it was getting dark and he was standing in the shadows, dressed in black.

"Where were you?" he asked, not exactly reproachful, but concerned.

"We went riding."

"We told you not to leave the property." That vein in his forehead was pulsing again.

"We didn't. I know the limits and we went nowhere near them," Eric assured him.

"Thank you." It sounded difficult for Gabriel to get out.

"I'll maybe see you tomorrow?" Eric asked me with a smile.

"Maybe," I agreed, smiling back. Eric went to Charlie's, and I headed to the villa, leaving Gabriel outside to do God-knows-what in the shadows.

CHAPTER NINE

"Aim for the pads," Sam told me, holding them up to his chest so I could practice my jabs, my cross, and my hook, like Caleb taught me at the beginning of the summer.

"You have to follow them, Ladybug, the enemy won't stay still for you." He brought his arms out to the side and above my head, so high that I couldn't reach.

"I'm not tall enough," I argued, jumping as high as I could, but not touching him. Not even close.

"Find something to help you then. You won't always be evenly matched, and I can't be there to help you."

Of course not. You died. The thought came into my mind, but I pushed it away. Sam wasn't dead, he was right in front of me, training me like they should have my whole life, to prepare me for what we were up against.

"There's nothing here," I said instead. We were in a field with tall grass. It was the perfect summer day, with not a cloud in the sky...but there wasn't any sun either. The light was white and artificial.

It felt like he kept getting taller and taller, so his head was further and further away from me. I looked around again, but couldn't see anything I could use to get higher, until Beth showed up out of nowhere.

"Beth!" I exclaimed. "Do you have a spell or something I can use? Maybe a ladder?" I asked, showing her how tall Sam was.

"You have everything you need," she said with a smile and a wink before walking over to me and crouching down, so I could get on her shoulders.

"Are you sure?" I must be pretty heavy.

"I've got you," she said with confidence.

I climbed on and let her straighten up, which gave me a few extra feet, but it wasn't enough. I looked down, about to tell her we needed more height, but I recognized Cassandra walking over and crouching down, like Beth had. I was sure I couldn't stay on, that there was no way the three of us could stand on top of each other without toppling over, but we did. I was almost there, so I tried extending my arms, but I couldn't reach.

By now I was expecting it when Rosalind ran over and crouched down. I wasn't even surprised when Annabelle came and managed to carry us all on her shoulders, making me at least four heads taller than Sam, who smiled.

"You figured it out."

"I had help," I argued, bringing my gloves to his pads, as he slowly regressed to his normal size.

The world was beautiful from up so high, and I felt like I could do anything, but as 'our enemy' grew smaller, the girls relieved their charges, one by one.

Once I was on solid ground, back to my own height, my ancestors smiled at me and walked off into the field they came from.

"Wait!" I called after them, but only Annabelle looked back at me and smiled, none of them even slowing down.

"They did what they needed to." Sam shrugged, taking off the pads.

"Will they come back?"

"I guess if you need them to."

"I need all the help I can get right now."

"You're living the adventure we dreamed about."

"Not like this," I argued. "It was supposed to be scary and thrilling, with magical creatures, pirates, and happy endings."

"You can't tell if the ending is happy until you reach it."

"When did you start talking like this?" I asked instead of telling him that the ending couldn't be happy if he wasn't there.

"When I became a grown-up." He ruffled my hair.

"I miss how easy it was when the manor was my playground and I was cute, so you followed me around and played all my games. Your mom made us cookies and ice cream, both if I was sad..."

"You were an annoying little monster." He was clearly lying and couldn't keep a straight face.

"You loved me."

"Still do," he assured me, as the clouds moved overhead. I looked up to see if the sun was still there, but when I came back down, we were in the parking lot at the motel.

"Sam, we need to go." I felt a chill and knew in my bones that something terrible was about to happen. I looked around in fear for Donovan and his followers to pounce on us. "Sam!" I turned and his throat was slit, with blood pouring out of it.

"Lucy," he struggled. "What did you do?"

"No, I didn't want this to happen, I tried to..."

"How could you?" he asked, clutching his throat before falling to the ground.

"Everyone you love dies," Donovan came out of nowhere and spat, less than an inch from my face.

I SCREAMED and woke up in a room I didn't recognize, with sweat pouring off me. I pulled the covers up to my chin and tried to breathe, reminding myself I was in Embry's house in

New Orleans, and it was just a nightmare. My breathing came back to normal as Gabriel rushed in, but the pain in my heart remained. The part that made the dream a nightmare was the part that really happened.

"Do you hear that?" I asked as Embry ran into the room, holding a baseball bat. I saw that Gabriel had discarded a fire poker when he found me alone in the room.

"It was just a nightmare," Embry said, sitting on the bed with me.

"I know. I'm sorry I woke you, but…that's my name." I wasn't sure at first, but I could hear it as clearly as Embry's words. Someone outside the window was calling my name.

"Is Charlie's grandson…" Gabriel sounded like he was ready to have some very unpleasant words with Eric if he was the cause of my nocturnal turmoil.

"No, it sounds like…" I stopped myself. It didn't make any sense. They would think I was crazy.

"It sounds like what?" Embry asked, but the sound was already growing faint. With the lights on and the guys there, I could almost convince myself I imagined it.

"It sounded like Sam calling me," I admitted, hating the look they exchanged, full of pity and concern.

"You don't hear it anymore?" Gabriel asked gently.

"Not as clearly."

"What was the nightmare?" Embry kept his hand on mine to help me calm down.

"It was just a weird dream with Sam." I knew how it sounded. "But then he died, and it was my fault, and he was so hurt."

"Sam knows it wasn't your fault and doesn't blame you," Embry told me.

"No, the real Sam doesn't know or feel anything, because he's dead." I knew he was trying to help, but this wasn't something I wanted to feel better about.

"Pancakes?" Gabriel asked, making Embry and I both look at him like he was crazy. "Unless you would rather go back to sleep, but it's 4 a.m., I'm up, and I'm hungry."

Embry looked at me to assess how I was feeling, so I shrugged. "I'm not getting back to sleep any time soon."

"I'll get them started."

There was one other time Gabriel made me pancakes in the middle of the night, although if memory served, they were actually crepes. Clara had this freak fever, and I can't remember where Embry was, but Sam wanted someone to stay with me at the plantation so I wouldn't catch it, and Gabriel was the one who showed up. I was not happy and wanted nothing more than to be back with Sam and Deanna, helping them take care of Clara. I would sing to her until she fell asleep, and hold her hand, so I spent the night on the couch, convinced they were going to call for me. When Gabriel realized I wasn't sleeping, he made crepes and we had one of those rare times where it's the middle of the night and he talks to me.

Part of me expected Embry to go back to bed so it would be like last time, but I knew that wasn't going to happen when I was this upset.

IT WAS hot in the house because Embry didn't believe in air conditioning unless it was so hot there was a chance we would melt. Still, I felt a chill, so I brought the quilt from the bed down with me.

"Do you want to take out the toppings?" Gabriel asked me while he worked the griddle.

"I'll set the table," Embry volunteered.

I took out peanut butter, Nutella, cinnamon, sugar, bananas, strawberries, lemon, cheese, and apples, then got chopping and slicing.

"What kind of toppings are these?" Embry asked once the table was set.

"It's the middle of the night so I didn't know if dessert pancakes or apple-cheese pancakes were more appropriate," I explained.

"You're adorable." Embry shook his head and started chopping the strawberries for me.

Soon enough we had a pile of crepes and a table covered with possible toppings.

"Delicious," I said once I bit into my apple-cheddar crepe. I coaxed Gabriel into letting me put the toppings on while it was still in the pan, so my cheese was all melty.

"I thought you were starting with your savory one?" Embry asked when I put maple syrup on it.

"Don't knock it until you've tried it," I warned.

"Why are you wasting your time being smart when you could be a chef?" Gabriel had copied me, and clearly approved.

"You're both crazy." Embry stuck to lemon and sugar. He sometimes splurged on a strawberry Nutella one, because he knew how good it was, but he was a traditionalist.

"Speaking of weird dreams..." Gabriel brought it back to what had us all awake at this ungodly hour.

"We weren't," I argued.

"Is that the first one?" Embry ganged up with him against me.

"I haven't had that particular dream before."

"But..." Gabriel caught on.

"But the ending is what I see all the time. Sometimes it plays over and over again and I can't make it stop," I admitted, using all my will to keep the tears in my eyes without letting them fall. I tried to make it sound like a minor annoyance, rather than something that kept me from sleeping most nights.

"You're right that we can't speak for Sam…" Embry said delicately, like they did every time they used his name around me. "But both of us would gladly give our final lives to keep you safe, without blaming anyone but the asshole who took them."

"My brain knows that. But he didn't give his life to save mine. He gave it because I chose not to go with Donovan. His death didn't change anything. They still kidnapped me, and then I got away. Maybe if I had gone willingly, I still would have escaped, but I wasn't brave enough to take that chance."

"You had no way of knowing what would happen. The potential consequences of giving Donovan what he wants are much greater," Gabriel insisted.

"And now that I have this magic thing that came out of nowhere…maybe I could have saved him. Instead of being selfish and scared for my own life, I could have tried to protect his. Instead of killing a woman to save myself, I could have evaporated Donovan to save Sam."

"This is why you don't sleep at night?" Gabriel was full of empathy, which somehow made it worse.

"I sleep," I argued. "Just not easily and not well."

"I wouldn't want you to be feeling this bad over it for me," Embry tried to reassure me with more things Sam could no longer do.

"Even if you had a wife and a daughter who didn't get to say goodbye, who would never see you again?" I admitted what weighed on me the most. My brain understood that Sam knew what would happen and still told me to go for it, but Deanna didn't expect to lose her husband for me. I was the reason Clara would grow up without her father.

"Sam didn't die because of you, Lucy, he died because of the kind of person he was. The kind who insisted on being your guardian and refused to let us take you, even when we told him all the dangers it entailed," Embry said with such conviction that I nearly believed him.

"That's another thing that scares me. I might not get the chance to have them yell at me and hate me, because they could be the next targets the Big Bad decides to use against me." I was failing to keep the tears from falling, but I fervently wiped them away as if that would prevent anyone from knowing they were there.

"They're safe," Gabriel assured me.

"Just because we know they're at the Beach House doesn't mean they're safe," I argued.

"I don't just know where they are, Luce. We have codes and signs to keep in touch. There's something Deanna can do that would alert people we trust if something was wrong. Help would be there within minutes of her doing it. We have people watching the house, watching the town. And she checks in every three days to let us know they're okay."

"Every three days?"

"Without fail," he agreed. "It's not like a phone call where we talk and ask questions, but the last one was yesterday, and everything was good."

"And you know for sure that it was her, not someone trying to keep up appearances?"

"I do."

"Have you read the book Ingrid left you?" Embry asked me, completely changing the subject.

"The first few pages," I played along.

"If it's the book I think it is, that's the one that tells you how to track essences, rather than a location on the map. You could see what they're doing rather than where they are."

"The one you said was dangerous?" I asked Gabriel.

"For Donovan, yes, but we can work on it today for people you care about," Embry took the lead.

CHAPTER TEN

We lasted until ten a.m. before I fell asleep on the swing with Ingrid's book, not long after Embry tipped his hat over his eyes and drifted off in the field. Luckily, my dreams were just dreams, that didn't make sense, but didn't upset me either.

When I woke up, I was lying on the swing with a blanket over me and Ingrid's book on the table beside me. I looked around, confused because Embry fell asleep before I did, but then I saw Gabriel a few feet away, keeping guard.

"Do you always take turns sleeping?" I asked, not ready to be awake yet.

"I'm not tired." He held in a yawn, which made his face look ridiculous and revealed his lie. "At night, inside the house, we take precautions so there's less of an overlap, but outside, when the rest of the world is awake and plotting, I would rather not chance it." He tried to say it in a nonchalant way so I wouldn't feel like I was in danger, but it was ever-present.

"I can keep watch if you want to take a nap," I offered, yawning with a stretch. I wasn't sure if I was ready to face the day or to go back to sleep.

"I'm good," he assured me with a smile.

"I know I'm not useful yet, but I can definitely manage to wake you if someone shows up," I defended myself.

"You're incredibly useful, Lucy, don't sell yourself short."

"True, an entire league of super soldiers wants to use me to take over the world."

"You're useful alive too," he told me. "There's more to you than looking like Annabelle."

I wanted to ask him what the more was, but he was looking at me in that intense way that made my heart beat faster and my cheeks flush.

"I'm thinking I should get a tattoo and cut my hair in a really weird way," I said instead.

"They know what you look like. A haircut won't trick them," Gabriel argued. "Unless you were planning on a face tattoo?" He kept his distance and would lean back as if he wanted to end the conversation, but then he would lean in again.

"Face and neck," I played along. "That way I'm unrecognizable from the front and the back."

"Not the craziest idea I've heard." He leaned back and got comfortable. "What would you get?"

"The face is hard, because it has to be big, and my mouth and eyes have to fit into it, but I feel like skeletons and spiderwebs are overdone…"

"People actually do that to themselves willingly?" he stopped me, leaning close.

"They do." I laughed. "And in the back, either a rainbow or a skull with crisscrossed bones."

"Please elaborate," he asked of me.

"Depending on the face, I either need the rainbow to tone it down, or the skull to ensure no one will ever approach me."

"I'm not sure a face tattoo would be enough of a deterrent."

"Paired with my personality?" I used self-deprecation because he wasn't teasing anymore.

"You don't stand a chance at scaring people away once they actually get to know you." I swallowed, feeling my heart pound before he went on. "You need to scare them away before they can get close." His eyes lingered on me.

"Hey, you're awake!" Eric interrupted, causing Gabriel to retreat, the moment gone.

"You saw me sleeping?" I asked, putting on a smile, but I couldn't help but wish he had come by a few minutes later.

"I saw you out here earlier. I wanted to see if you were up for a ride, but you were snoring."

"I don't snore," I argued, though I didn't really have a clue.

"Don't worry, it was cute." He smiled before looking awkwardly to Gabriel, kind of nervous. We weren't technically kids, but the guys gave off a vibe that told people to stay away from me.

"Don't mind me, I was just leaving." Gabriel got up, but he looked at Eric in a way that made him even more nervous.

"I think we were supposed to work on stuff," I argued, nodding towards Ingrid's book.

"Embry can help you with that when you get back. You two should go have fun." Gabriel walked off, but it was weird. I felt like I did something wrong, or I upset him, and I didn't like it.

"Did you not want to come?" Eric looked at me expectantly.

"A ride sounds perfect," I assured him, heading for the stables.

I CHOSE Donner again and got him saddled, then Eric mostly let me lead. I think he felt that I was in a weird place and needed to clear my mind, because there was a lot of galloping, and I was out of breath by the time we got back around mid-afternoon.

"It's like you've been riding your whole life." Eric smiled while he unsaddled Rudolph and I brushed Donner.

"I had an excellent teacher and an amazing horse."

"You can also take credit."

"I do, when it's deserved," I assured him.

"You're pretty special, Lucy Owens."

"Thank you, Eric…Finch?"

"Finch," he agreed.

"I didn't even know your last name."

"Don't sweat it, you know the important stuff."

"Like your favorite Care Bear?" I brought up one of the random things I knew about him. Daydream Bear for him, Grams Bear for me.

"It doesn't get more personal than that," he teased. "Although it's a lot easier to find people with last names."

"Find them…" I pressed, my brain going straight to the people hunting me.

"You know, after you go home, when you realize you miss me." He got a huge smile that I couldn't help but reciprocate.

"Yes, last names would help at that point."

I shook my head at him before Embry walked over, smiling at the two of us.

"Ready to try some stuff?" he asked me, holding Ingrid's book.

"Time for your daily homework I guess." Eric sounded disappointed. He always called it my homework. We never openly discussed magic, the Gifted, or any of that stuff around him, so I couldn't tell if he was oblivious and really thought we were doing quizzes and science experiments every day. The guys were overprotective and could be overbearing, but I doubt either of them really cared how well I did in school. Especially since it was highly unlikely I would ever step foot in a Harvard classroom. I winced, trying not to think about what this year was supposed to look like.

"We won't be too long. You can probably have her for supper."

I turned to Embry, not sure what was going on, but he gave me a head nod and something resembling a wink.

"Then I guess I'll see you later, Miss Owens," Eric said before heading to Charlie's.

I FOLLOWED Embry to the other side of the barn, where the blanket was already laid out on the ground.

"What do we need for this one?" I asked, seeing nothing but the checkered picnic blanket.

"Nothing but you," he said simply. "Even for the other tracking spell, all you really need is the crystal, the string, and the map. The rest was to make you feel like you weren't on your own, but you just need a clear picture of the person you're scrying for. Most of the words to these simple spells become superfluous when you know what you're doing. It's all about intention."

"I will things to happen?" I severely doubted his assessment of my skills.

"There's a little more finesse to it. It's not like you can will yourself to win the lottery or fly, but things don't happen because you channel a candle's energy or say something in Latin...they happen because you set the intention for them to," he explained.

"Ingrid's book has pages of instructions. It would be way lighter if all you needed was intent."

"There are methods to help channel your intentions. I'm not knocking them. I'm saying the way it worked for Beth, and seems to work for you, is that you don't need that extra boost."

"No pressure." I sighed.

"I don't want you to be somewhere and need to use a spell but hold back because you don't have the right crystal," he explained his insistence.

"Didn't it also say I needed something from the person I was tracking?" I asked, mentally going through the pages on tracking people. I saw them in my head like chemistry labs; a set of ingredients and the steps you take to combine them into something better. It was pretty easy to figure out what ingredients were used to boost the magic signal, but I felt like the object of the person you're tracking was essential to not track the wrong person.

"You have your ring, so we can start with Clara." He sat on the blanket. "But I'm pretty sure it will work without objects for people you have a strong emotional connection to."

"Only love, or fear and hatred too?" I thought of Donovan, not wanting any kind of connection to him.

"I wouldn't use this version for someone you didn't feel positively towards. My car broke down when I was driving back from a trip to see Caleb and Etta, so Beth got worried. She used this tracking spell and... I don't have powers, so I didn't know exactly what was going on, but it was like I could feel her in my heart and all around me. Not in an overwhelming way, but I think that if I was someone who did have powers and wanted to hurt her, it could have been dangerous."

"What exactly am I doing?"

"Why don't we try with Clara, then you can tell me if you want to use it for other people, or Donovan," he suggested.

"Is it safe?" I was nervous now.

"For Clara, it should be." I trusted him more than anything in this world, but the magic...not so much.

We opened Ingrid's book to the appropriate page, and I closed my eyes. I slid the ring into the palm of my hand and held it, picturing Clara laughing as she dragged me through the garden, wanting to show me some creature she discovered, or a fort she built us in the trees. It was all so real that I could hear her laughing outside my head, then everything changed.

It was like I suddenly zoomed in on her from outer space.

She was building a sandcastle on a somewhat deserted beach, wearing a bright yellow swimsuit with an overly large sunhat.

"It's not a real cake because it's made out of sand," Clara explained, checking on the mounds she laid out on the rocks behind her to cook in the sun. "Maybe we can make real ones after supper, with sprinkles, and I can lick the spoons?"

"Only if you eat all your food," Deanna warned, but she was smiling.

"We can keep some for daddy and Lucy," Clara tried, keeping her head down, but bringing her eyes up to see Deanna's reaction.

"It's not like we can eat all the cupcakes ourselves," Deanna agreed, but I felt like her smile was forced. Thinking of Sam broke her heart as much as it did mine.

"So?" Embry asked when I came back to him.

"It was like I was there and felt her. She was making sand-castles and... I could feel the sand, and the warmth of her sun." It sounded crazy, even to me, but crazy was relative these days.

"That's how Beth described it," he agreed. "She said it was like—"

"Like a part of me went to her," I finished for him.

"She said a part of her essence, but yes."

"I would never want to do that for Donovan." I shivered just thinking about it.

"That was my assumption."

"How does it feel for Clara?" I asked, not wanting her to freak out as he had described for himself.

"Like a hug."

"From me, or from someone?"

"I felt like it was from Beth, but I might have made the assumption based on the limited number of people who felt that way about me and could do magic."

.   .   .

WE DID IT A FEW TIMES, so I got to see Deanna making brownies with Clara, and Keisha working on a research paper, before Embry called it a day.

"What are our dinner plans?" I asked when he said I was free to go.

"I didn't have any, but it sounded like you and Eric…"

"He's nice, but I don't know how much he knows about me, if I can trust him, or if getting close to him just puts him in danger," I admitted.

"Charlie knows. And it's not like we hide when we practice," he pointed out.

"Why are you so invested in this *relationship?*"

"Because you're a Bearer of the Crescent Moon, but you're also a teenage girl who just graduated from high school and deserves to have some fun with someone her own age and be reminded what she's fighting for."

"Why are you acting like we're safe here? Just because we got rid of Gabriel's tracker…"

"Because of Beth." He sighed, another memory making him sad. "She made sure this property was safe for her friends, for me, and in case someone ever came after her family. Cloaking, warnings, places where magic doesn't work…she thought of everything."

"I thought magic disappeared when the person who did it…" I couldn't say the words to him, but I could vividly see the sink going back to its original state when the woman died.

"Some of it does," he agreed. "Donovan's control, my mood swings…they end as soon as we do. But if Etta heals you, you're healed. Some magic lingers…"

"How do you know which is which?"

"You don't. But then again, once she heals you, the wound is gone. I need proximity to alter your mood, and Donovan needs a bond to control someone…they're temporary in nature."

"But the protective spells are permanent?"

"The important ones are," he assured me.

I BROUGHT Ingrid's book back to my room, but when I came downstairs, Embry and Gabriel were having a heated argument in the kitchen.

"What do *you* know about it?" Gabriel's voice carried with anger and indignation. "Just because you inserted yourself into her life doesn't give you the right…"

I tried to mind my own business and not listen, but I could feel that this fight was a long time coming and there would be consequences. I debated walking in and interrupting them, but waited in the living room instead. Hopefully, it was the type of thing you had to get out, so you could get over it.

"You don't understand, Embry. You have no idea what you're talking about."

"I love her, and I will not let you—" Embry fumed.

"Let me?"

It wasn't that I was eavesdropping, because I tried to tiptoe to the door, but it was hard not to hear their angry whispers. They were talking over each other, so I got the tone more than the words, until Eric showed up and they stopped, leaving an awkward silence until Eric asked if he should come back later.

I hid behind the staircase a second before Gabriel barged in and stormed off through the front door. I heard the car start and wanted to run after him and beg him not to leave, but all I could do was hope he would come back. I got that it was upsetting to have your best friend fall in love with your fiancée when the two of them thought you were dead, but it happened over three centuries ago. It was time to move on.

CHAPTER ELEVEN

Gabriel eventually came back, but he and Embry avoided each other like the plague. As soon as one of them walked into a room the other was in, they would look really annoyed, then leave.

I tried talking to both of them individually, to make them see how ridiculous they were being, but the daggers their eyes shot told me to mind my own business.

It was a relief by the time Wednesday came and Embry said I was still going to Ingrid's shop. I was hoping they would put aside their differences and go together to protect me better, but they made up some excuse as to why it was smarter to take two separate cars. I rode with Embry, and Gabriel followed us incognito-style, so it was like he wasn't even there.

"You know you can tell him about Beth and the fight would be over. You guys could kiss and make up for centuries of—"

"It isn't about Beth," Embry argued.

"Not directly, but—"

"Maybe it's time he gets off his high horse and sees that my mistake doesn't give him the right to go around for centuries hurting people and toying with their emotions," he said before taking a breath that was full of regret. "I didn't mean that, I'm just upset."

"I think it's also a mistake that you were married at least five years and didn't tell him. Whether it was to an Owens woman or some random girl out there, if I was him, I would be hurt about that," I pointed out.

"He stopped being my best friend centuries before my wedding."

"How did you guys manage to raise Margaret together?" It felt like they mostly survived my childhood by spending limited amounts of time together, running off to do their own things once the big moments were done, and only talking to each other about me.

"It was like when parents stay together for the kids. Regardless of how we felt, Maggie needed us, so we were there for her."

"But I'm not a kid anymore?" I asked of the sudden change in their behavior.

"No, you're not." He looked pointedly at me, then shook his head and let out a breath.

"Funny how you can make me a child or an adult at whim, depending on which way you need the conversation to go."

"You're not a kid who can be fooled by us getting along. By the time Margaret was sixteen, we would take turns going on business trips, and she knew exactly why."

"She knew why you didn't like each other?" I doubted it.

"She knew it was to avoid each other, but we managed to keep the why out of it. For all his hating me, he never wanted her to."

"Yeah, sounds like he hates you," I said sarcastically, looking out the window to try and see Gabriel in my side mirror. When I gave up and looked back at Embry, he had a tiny smile.

"We've been through a lot." He sighed. "And even though we've spent way more time not liking each other than we did as best friends, that's still how I see him."

"But…" I saw it coming.

"But this won't be fixed by an apology. It's not just *him* who is mad at *me* this time. He has things to answer for as well."

"And will you tell him that?"

"No," he told me.

"That's why I still meddle, even when you tell me not to."

"I know," he assured me.

THE STORE WAS CLOSED when we got there, but Embry knocked so Ingrid, looking about my age, could come and let us in.

"Perfect! You're just in time," she said, ushering me in. "You can come to get her around four o'clock," she added for Embry.

"We don't leave her alone," he argued.

"This is why children rebel and hitchhike across the country," she warned him.

"I'll take my chances."

"TV's upstairs, but don't touch my peanut butter squares." She held out a finger at him.

"Wouldn't dream of it." He took a staircase behind a wall of beads I would never have known was there.

"Just in time for what?" I asked. She ushered me to the back room she'd come out of the first time I met her. I hesitated a bit in the doorway before following her in.

At first, I couldn't see with the dim lighting and the smoke that made me cough, but my eyes adjusted so I could see the large iron cauldron over a fire in the middle of the room.

"Seriously?" If Embry didn't trust her so much, and I hadn't seen her magic with my own eyes, I would have assumed she was a fraud who watched too many movies.

"A friend brought her kids, so I put on a little show for them. It's a genuine cauldron, but there's nothing but spaghetti sauce inside."

"Genuine cauldron as in…"

"As in it's ancient, from Salem, but ninety-nine percent of the witches murdered there couldn't do magic to save their lives, so in this case genuine means it's really old."

"Do you know which ones could?" I asked of the Salem witches, wondering if there was a secret directory or something in the Wiccan community.

"Annabelle was, wasn't she? At least that's what Beth told me. Most real witches knew better than to get caught, and if they did, they could get out of it."

"You weren't…" I let the thought linger, but her smile told me she understood.

"I was born the same year as Beth. I just find it fascinating." She got a dreamy look. "There'll be time for questions later; I want you to see the bloom." She brought me to another room that was like a greenhouse with special lighting, misters, and temperature controls. It looked more like an illegal drug operation than the back room of an apothecary.

She brought me to the end of the room, where a large potted plant had a single bulb in the middle.

"Take this and hold it here." She handed me what looked like a miniature pewter cauldron, filled with a foul-smelling orange liquid.

"Are you sure it's blooming today?" I didn't see any sign of movement or growth in the bulb.

"Any minute now." She smiled, with scissors in her hands. "Keep it steady," she warned, eyeing the mini cauldron.

I did as I was told, though I didn't see the point, until the bulb suddenly came to life. The green pulled back, petal by petal, slowly revealing a beautiful flower of deep red and magenta. It was mesmerizing, but just as it reached what I felt was its full potential, Ingrid used the scissors to cut the flower off and let it fall into the mini-cauldron I held steady.

"What was that for?" I was upset that she killed it before it even had a chance to fully bloom, after making such a fuss about it.

"The potion you are holding takes a month to mature and is good for less than three days before you need a new one. The Cereus Labilis blooms once every year for mere seconds, but the flower is the pivotal ingredient in the potion. The fuller the better, but if I cut after it starts to close, I have to start all over and buy a new plant," she explained.

"What does the potion do?" It sounded complex.

"Numbs the heart," she said dismissively.

"That doesn't sound good." The guys said Etta could heal everything except a broken heart, which told me there was a reason why that shouldn't be done. You have to let time slowly fit the pieces back together.

"It isn't. But when you lose a child and still have another one to take care of, you need something to get through the day."

"Do you usually sell ingredients, or full potions?"

"Most of my clients dabble for fun, so they get the ingredients, the cauldrons, and the crystals and they feel more in control of their destinies. A lot will come here to replenish their stores of particular items, while others will only come to me for something incredibly complicated, with dire consequences if they mess up."

"Like this one," I understood. "Potions are your strong suit?"

"I can alter what you see better than anyone, but my other magic is amateur at best. Beth usually did the spells and let me mix the potions."

"You were in a coven together?"

"We were best friends. We did everything together." She gave me a sad smile.

"Do you know what it is you're meant to do?" I asked delicately. While some might see it as a chance to live forever and be invincible, I got the feeling Ingrid was anxious to move on.

"Rule the world," she teased, unaware that it was not a

laughing matter for me. "There are people who are in the right place at the right time, while others have skills and a drive that compels them to do something. For me, that's potions. I assume I will invent a formidable potion someday. Or use a normal one to save someone formidable."

"But you won't know if you got it until you don't come back."

"I'll know when I turn nine," she argued.

"What do you mean?"

"In my very limited experience, dying before you achieve your purpose brings you back and stops time where your body is concerned, preserving you to that moment in time. I believe that once you do what you're supposed to, time starts again, and you live the normal life you should have."

"You start over?" I asked, thinking of Gabriel and Embry.

"I'll be me, with all my years and experiences, but I'll be able to turn eighteen and date a man who can actually see me, rather than what I imagine I would look like at that age."

"Do all your customers know…"

"Most don't." She shook her head. "I age until I turn thirty or so, mention a niece or a daughter, take some time off to 'die', then come back as someone new." She used air quotations when she said 'die', like it was a dirty word.

"Is Ingrid your…" I knew it was what Beth called her at least.

"My real name," she agreed. "Most people call me Ivy currently."

"I.V." I remembered the sign. "But Mr. Fraser—-"

"It's nice to have someone you can be yourself with. When we're alone, I call him John," she assured me.

"This is for the mother of the boy who disappeared?" The potion turned a deep purple.

"Aye, but they found Billy."

"I can't imagine what she's going through." I was used to

losing people, but that didn't make it any easier. And I'm not sure I could recover from losing Clara.

"Someone drowned him in the swamps. It was so shallow that a person would have to choke you out or hold your head under." She shivered and wrapped her shawl tighter around her body.

"I'm so sorry," I told her.

"Not as sorry as whoever did it will be." I didn't necessarily feel unsafe, but there was a dark focus to her actions. I wouldn't want to cross her. "How did you like the book?" She changed the subject.

"Very interesting. I had this weird dream, so Embry suggested I use your tracking spell to make sure my family was okay. I liked that."

"What kind of weird dream?" She perked up.

"I saw someone die, so I see it happen when I close my eyes sometimes." I tried to make it not sound weird and depressing, but she looked at me like she knew it wasn't only sometimes, or just someone.

"What was weird about it?" She stopped what she was doing with the potion to look at me.

"I felt like he was calling me." I shrugged. It was less weird than the human pyramid, but it was Sam's voice in the middle of the night that stayed with me.

"In your dream?" she asked, going to a bookshelf.

"More like after I woke up," I admitted. "No one else heard it." I felt fairly confident she wasn't going to lock me up for hearing things.

"They aren't usually this active…" she said, mostly to herself.

"What are we talking about?"

"The fee follet." She finally looked up to me.

"Of course." Like that made any sense.

"You're staying at Beth's?"

"Yes, but what are fee follet?"

"They're fairies." She brought the book over to me. "Louisiana's version of a siren. They appear as a floating light and call out to you. Instead of luring sailors into the rocks, they lure people into the swamps."

"This happened before?"

"It's usually one or two people every decade, although they're more active during great wars or epidemics."

"Did a big tragedy happen recently?" I asked.

"No, which is why I didn't consider them before. But if you heard them calling you…"

"I did."

"I'll look into it," she assured me.

"Is there anything I can do?"

"Whip me up a sleeping draught."

"Are you having trouble sleeping?"

"For you," she corrected. "To learn, not take, unless you feel like you need it. Some potions require more than mixing the right ingredients in the proper way. Others, like this draught, demand finesse. I have half a dozen we should get through before Embry takes you back."

By late afternoon, Ingrid had guided me through the steps of making a sleeping draught, truth serum, an antidote to most common poisons, a love spell, a focusing draught, and one that burns like acid, but doesn't hurt skin.

"A love spell?" Embry asked while we drove home, and I gave him a recap of my day.

"She says it's temporary. It lasts six hours if ingested, but you can get ten minutes or so if you throw it at them."

"How would that help anyone?"

"It wouldn't if my goal was for them to love me forever, but if someone bad captured me, I could maybe convince them to let me escape. It would at least give me a couple of minutes head start."

"She's...special, but she knows what she's doing. I've seen her get out of impossible situations with mostly her wits," Embry said fondly.

"And magic."

"No, I think she was worse during the summer she chose not to use magic. Helen was eight, and just lost her mother, so Ingrid thought it would be fun to really bond with her goddaughter. I think she wanted to stop hiding for a while as well. She was a force to be reckoned with."

I finished off by telling him about the fee follet, and how worried Ingrid seemed to be about them, before we pulled into the driveway, closely followed by Gabriel. I wondered what he did in town all day, or if he was only with us for the drives.

CHAPTER TWELVE

On Friday morning, Embry left early under the pretense of running errands. I'm pretty sure he was just spending the day at Charlie's so I could have some time with Gabriel. Which was considerate, but I'd much rather they end their centuries-long grudge.

Gabriel got back from his run as I was putting my cereal bowl into the dishwasher.

"Would you like some coffee?" I asked after he took off his headphones. Running turned me into a sweating mess, where my hair went frizzy, and my skin got blotchy; it wasn't pretty. Gabriel, on the other hand, was glistening and tan from the sun, so he looked like the statue of a Greek God, rather than a hot mess. It was unnerving.

"I would love some, thank you," he said before going up the stairs, presumably to shower.

I used the French press and ground some beans to be fancy, while making myself an Earl Grey tea. I made a lot of it, and I made it strong, in the hopes of adding ice to it later. The sweet tea here was amazing, but I was craving something with less sugar.

"Are you ready?" Gabriel asked, coming over and taking a sip of the coffee I made. He ran his hand through his hair, shaking it to remove the excess water.

"Coming." I took my tea and followed him to the blanket we always practice on.

"WHAT AM I LEARNING TODAY?" I was able to track people on a map, make small objects float, and make things temporarily catch fire, even without a candle. Luckily, it was a safe fire that didn't burn you when you touched it, because my instinct the first few times was to send it away from myself, which usually meant throwing it straight at Gabriel.

"I thought we would try a few of these." He opened the Book of Shadows to pages with dark borders. I had ignored them ever since I saw the picture of an invisible hand choking a woman on the first one.

"Or we could see if I can levitate."

"You can." He motioned to the rock I'd overturned.

"Myself," I argued.

"That would definitely be very cool, but I don't think it would be useful."

"Probably not against the Big Bad, but for day-to-day chores, grabbing things off high shelves...very useful."

"Cute," he assured me. "But I thought you wanted us to train you so the next time they find us you won't be defenseless."

"That's true," I agreed. "But if I never use them, what's the point in learning them?"

"Why wouldn't you use them?"

"Because I don't really trust the magic yet, and those spells look like something I don't want to accidentally use on the wrong person or go too far."

"We can start small then, see if you get comfortable, and stop whenever you want," he offered.

"Okay."

HE WENT through the book and found a page he thought fit the criteria. It had ropes drawn around the text, but closer inspection revealed that it would immobilize someone, as if they were held in place by ropes.

"Useful but doesn't harm." He waited for my reaction.

"What should I practice on?" I looked around for a bag of potatoes or something. "The scarecrow?" I asked of the tiny, doll-like figure out in the distance of Charlie's yard.

"You won't know if it works unless you try it on something that moves."

"We can go to the swamps Eric takes me to. They're full of mosquitoes," I suggested.

"You can practice on me." He turned my idea down.

"What if I do it wrong and hurt you?"

"I trust you," he assured me, but I was still nervous. "I'll just come back," he teased, trying to make me smile, but I wasn't there yet. "You've got this, Lucy. I promise." He took my hands in his to support his claim, but I could feel my heart beating faster and my cheeks going red from his touch.

I reread the page in question, which didn't have an incantation, just advice on things I could say to focus my powers, and the intention I needed to have. It was great that Annabelle and Beth had so much faith in their powers and intentions, but what if I was distracted or my mind wandered, and I did something terrible? What if I ended up doing one of the other things from those pages, with much scarier images of missing limbs and storm clouds?

"Are you okay to try it once?" he asked after a couple of minutes.

"Sure," I said, feeling anything but.

Gabriel walked towards me, slowly, so I concentrated on

stopping him. I imagined invisible ropes around his arms and legs, keeping him in place.

"I'm sorry," I said when he reached me without anything happening.

"You don't have to apologize."

"I tried," I told him.

"But..." he said like he already knew the answer.

"I don't want to hurt you. I don't want to concentrate too hard and stop more than your limbs, or think of something or someone else and..."

"I get it."

"You're upset."

"I'm not," he assured me.

"You wanted me to learn all their magic and I'm not making it easy."

"The magic isn't for me," he said, taken aback.

"Embry?" Now I was confused.

"You say you want to fight Donovan and the Big Bad next time they come."

"We can't keep running and letting them surprise us and take Sam," I agreed.

"How did you expect to do that? Martial arts and weapons?"

"It can't hurt, compared to not knowing anything to defend myself."

"I have seen Caleb go against them. I've had help from someone with blades at the end of their arms...Cassie was strong and fierce, and she had knowledge and weapons..."

"She gave up," I pointed out, which was clearly the wrong thing to say, because he glared at me as if I was the one who murdered her.

"She gave her life to protect her daughter," he argued. "And it was after a long time spent running away from them, and a terrible defeat."

"You let her fight them?"

"We didn't have a choice. He surprised us and we were never very good at getting Cassie to do anything she didn't want to." He got a sad smile as he remembered her. "The point is, I could train you in every weapon and every martial art I know, but I don't think any of that will make a difference. Because the real Big Bad, he doesn't need to touch you to kill you. He might not even need to be in the same room...I'm not saying this to scare you..."

"But I'm dead no matter what?" I let him know I understood.

"No." He was upset. "Weapons and combat won't defeat them, but you have something Cassie didn't. You have Annabelle's magic. The only reason I am pushing you to learn how to use it is that if I have to let you defend yourself against them, I need to give you a fighting chance."

"And you think these spells are my best chance to stay alive?"

"I do."

"I can't let them win." I sighed, resigning myself to being uncomfortable.

"And I can't lose you." He looked right at me as he said it, with an intensity that made me feel like he could hear how fast my heart was beating. "None of us are willing to accept that outcome." He turned away from me, but it took a while for my heart to go back to normal.

"Let's try again," I relented.

"I don't want to push you if it makes you uncomfortable. It's no use to us if you *can* do stuff to them but you're never actually going to use it."

"I'm nervous about my powers but you're right. I would rather learn how to use them, so I can focus and immobilize the next person who comes at me, instead of blowing them up." I took a deep breath, trying not to see that woman, or the pile she became when I was done with her.

"If it's Donovan, or the Big Bad, or anyone who is trying to hurt you, you do what you need to stay alive." he waited until I met his eyes, adding weight to each word.

"But hopefully it won't come to that?"

"If I had my way, you would never know about any of this. You would live your life and be happy and none of it would touch you." He got a dark, haunted look.

"Bad things happen even if there isn't a Big Bad hunting you down," I said simply.

"I would protect you from that stuff as well, if I could." His eyes locked with mine in a promise.

"I know. But it's not something anyone can protect me from." I shook my head to snap out of it. "Do I try it on you again?"

"Do your worst. I can handle it," he assured me with an uncharacteristic wink.

He started walking towards me, so I imagined the ropes binding around him and he stopped. It wasn't really like invisible ropes, because other than his eyes, he couldn't move anything. Not even to try and break free.

"It worked!" I said excitedly, but he was still frozen in place, so I imagined him walking to me again, which he did.

"That was perfect." He beamed.

WE WORKED on that a bit longer, then I tried to build an invisible barrier between us, so whatever he threw at me would bounce off.

"There has to be a way to combine both," I said after we were at it for hours. I could either make one that blocked his high-speed body from colliding with mine, or one that stopped objects he threw at me from getting through. The same barrier couldn't withstand weapons and magic. I had to let one fade away and conjure a new one, which was not an easy feat.

This was the first spell to take a lot out of me. I had to rest a bit between each attempt, or the barrier disappeared as soon as the first assault bounced off.

"What does the book say to do?"

"Imagine a shield for weapons, and a wall of energy for things with magic." I reread it every couple of tries to see if I was doing something wrong.

"Can you picture something in your mind that withstands both?"

"I could try." I shrugged.

"Go for it."

I imagined a wall of blue energy, like water, with a hard shell around it. Once I nodded to say I was ready, Gabriel threw a rock so it would hit above my head, but still within the force shield, and ran at me with his super speed. The rock hit and bounced back, so I closed my eyes to brace against the inevitable collision. I felt it happen, but it was a few feet ahead of me, where I had the shield.

I opened my eyes, ready to celebrate with Gabriel, but he was at least twenty feet away, on the ground, not moving.

"Gabriel!" I screamed, my heart in my throat, cursing away tears as I ran over. I shook him when I got there, praying I hadn't killed him.

What felt like an eternity later, but was probably only seconds, he woke up and coughed. The air was knocked out of him when he collided with my wall and bounced back into a willow tree.

"I thought I lost you. That I killed you." I tried to steady my breathing, holding on to his hand like an anchor.

"I'm fine," he assured me, struggling to get up.

"This is why I don't like the magic," I told him.

"Accidents happen, Lucy, it really wasn't that bad. With a bit of practice, you'll be able to--"

"No. You say that I need to practice so I can control it, but I've been practicing and I'm still hurting people."

"You need to give it time."

"No. I'm never doing that again." I crossed my arms, cold now that the fear adrenaline was wearing off.

"Lucy…"

"You said we could stop, and this makes me uncomfortable."

"Okay." He wasn't happy, but he didn't follow me as I went back to the villa, still shaking.

CHAPTER THIRTEEN

I woke up early the next morning and went for a jog. Staying on the property made it quite the workout, since I had to run through the wooded trails instead of flat roads. By the time I got back to the villa, I was exhausted and covered in sweat.

"What's with the new look?" Embry asked me, sitting at the kitchen table with his espresso.

I filled a large glass of water and drank it before answering him. "Working on my cardio." My breathing was still labored, but my heartbeat was slowly getting back to normal.

"Because you plan on listening next time we tell you to run?" he asked with the hint of a smile.

"Gabriel didn't tell you?" My legs were killing me, so I wanted nothing more than to take the seat next to him, but I knew from experience that I should keep moving, so I walked around the room instead.

"He hasn't." He raised an eyebrow at me.

"I've decided that I don't want to work on the magic anymore. I want you guys to train me like what we did at Caleb's. Kickboxing, weapon-wielding, throwing things…

anything I can use against Donovan's army." I looked him square in the eyes.

"What about Donovan?" he asked when his judgmental look didn't make me falter.

"You would never actually let me fight him. I'm not a match for him either way."

"Gabriel agreed to this?"

"He said I could stop with the magic."

"What happened? You were doing so good." He looked defeated.

"I was hurting people," I reminded him. "I practically set Gabriel on fire, nearly crushed the mole with that rock, and almost killed Gabriel when I threw him into a tree."

"None of those actually hurt anybody," Embry argued.

"I killed that woman in the diner. I'm sure she'd done terrible things, but there's a reason why we put people in jail and have trials before sentencing them to death. I didn't even know what I was doing. I raised my arms and she died. I don't ever want that to happen again."

He opened his mouth to say something, then looked at my face and reconsidered. "I won't force you to do something you don't want to do."

"Thank you." I took a seat beside him. "Will you train me?"

"I'll do everything in my power to make sure you make it through this." He put his hand on mine.

I SPENT my mornings training with Embry, alternating between kickboxing and fencing, then Gabriel would come in the afternoons and do some capoeira or aikido with me. We had just started hand-to-hand combat, and it was by far my favorite. I would say I was getting good at it, but learning the equivalent of a choreography with Gabriel was not the same thing as fighting an assailant who took me by surprise.

When Embry had asked me what I would feel most comfortable using if Donovan's people found us again I'd told him hand-to-hand, so I wasn't surprised when he showed up during my training session with Gabriel.

"Why are you hoping I'll be terrible at this?" I asked, knowing how upset he was that it was my favorite.

"Because if you're more confident in hand-to-hand combat, you're going to let them get close enough so you can use it, which isn't something we ever want to happen." They were united in their concern.

"Or I won't panic if someone happens to get close," I argued.

"In a crisis, we don't rise to the occasion, we fall back on our training," Gabriel said like a mantra, upping the speed of our training because I refused to stop and let them talk me down.

"We can keep working on the sticks and swords too," I assured them.

"Fencing doesn't count," Embry argued.

"Then why did you bother teaching it to me?" True, the fencing swords wouldn't be my first choice if I was attacked, but some of the skills had to be transferable to real swords.

"In an ideal world, they would never get close enough for you to use any of it."

"You're still planning on hiding me any time someone comes close to us? Spend the rest of my life running?"

"If you're using sticks and stones to fight them, then yes." At least Embry was apologetic.

"They won't be unarmed when they come for you, Lucy," Gabriel pointed out. We were in a groove, going faster and faster so I felt completely connected to him. Then he went faster than humanly possible and got my wrists in one hand behind my back, his other arm resting against my neck before I even knew what was going on. "They will have weapons you can see, Gifts that you can't, or both."

"But you can use this in the future, if there's a weird guy on campus or something," Embry tried to make me feel better as Gabriel released me, his point made.

"Do I even have a future? I either spend the rest of my life outrunning him, or he finds me and I'm dead."

"No," they said in unison, but neither had a plan nor reasoning as to why I would be different from all the Owens women before me.

"I know you think this is useless unless I'm going against a drunk college kid who isn't much taller or stronger than me," I summed up their concerns. "But I would like to have options if ever I am cornered with one of them again."

"You run," Gabriel said with an intensity that left no room for discussion.

"How about we call it a night?" Embry suggested.

"I'll go do some laps." I left them there and went to change into a bathing suit.

I WAS TRYING to make up for a lifetime of prioritizing book smarts in as little time as possible. My legs protested even light jogging this morning, but the water felt wonderful. I started out with the breaststroke, but mostly swam from one end to the other underwater. Adrenaline would help me go faster and harder, but learning to hold and control my breath would help keep me focused. Right now, I needed all the help I could get.

CHAPTER FOURTEEN

"It's a shame you can't see NOLA. You've been here for weeks, and you still haven't seen more than this place and one store in the Quarter," Eric said, leaning against the edge of the pool. When he found out about my new goal of 'becoming a fighting machine' as he called it, he offered to teach me a few things from his time on the wrestling team in high school. It gave me a new appreciation of why the guys were so worried about me getting close to someone in a fight. Not that I would admit it to them, but I had no interest in ever getting close enough to use wrestling. Unless it was a throw, after I got a lot better at them.

Once Eric ran through what he said were the absolute basics, we decided to go for a swim to rinse off the sweat, escape the heat, and enjoy his last day before going back to school.

"It's not really a sightseeing vacation," I defended.

"There's not sightseeing and then there's not leaving your hotel room," Eric argued.

"I'm sure you've noticed Embry and Gabriel are very over-protective."

"I have," he agreed with that smile. I was pretty sure he had every girl at Louisiana State drooling over him. Charlie either didn't let him out when he was here, or he came to get away from it all, because it did not make sense that he was spending all this time with me.

"What's the one thing I absolutely have to see?" I asked, making a mental list in case I made it out alive.

"Cafe du Monde," he said without hesitation.

"Out of all the history and culture in New Orleans, your recommendation is that I have a donut?" I verified.

"Beignets," he argued. "And I was mostly teasing, but they are delicious. And it's not that hard to get in and out of. What would you want to see, since you seem to know all about it?"

"Someday, if I come back, I would love to see Bourbon Street and Jackson Square. And do some ghost walks…but if you gave me an hour to explore right now, I would choose the library."

"You're one of those?" He shook his head like he should have known, and couldn't believe I fooled him.

"I am," I agreed. "But that's not why."

"The architecture?" he asked, not buying it.

"For starters, we don't have internet here."

"I can easily fix that."

"By choice," I stopped him. "But they also have the perfect combination of real books, and ones on fairytales."

"Are you saying fairytales aren't real? Or just the books that contain them?"

"They're real books, just not the published kind of book you would find on amazon." As I said it, I realized that was probably the exact kind of book you would find online, but I wanted a more reputable source than someone dabbling in witchcraft from their basement. I wanted the really old, authentic volumes with only a couple of copies buried in private libraries.

"How do you even know what's in our library?"

"Ingrid. She owns the store we went to in the Quarter." I asked her about it during my last visit. It apparently also housed a paranormal cookbook with killer muffins, and histories of witch trials, like the ones in Salem.

"There's a little library less than a mile from here."

"She mentioned it was in an old church…"

"At the fork in the road, under the oak trees," he finished for me.

"Have you been?"

"Not by choice." He smiled at my look of disappointment. "But I wouldn't mind bringing you to see it."

"Oh, you wouldn't mind?"

"Not one bit," he agreed.

"I doubt they'd let me go." I sighed.

"What if we got lost horseback riding?"

"Are you being a bad influence, Mr. Finch?"

"I'm trying to be the knight in shining armor who gets you to your library," he feigned innocence.

"Where exactly is it?"

"Across from the old well. If we cut through the woods, it's literally across the street."

"Literally?" I pressed. Most people these days used that word interchangeably with almost. Or figuratively.

"Cross my heart and hope to die."

"Let's not go that far." I bit my bottom lip, considering it. Now that I knew the Big Bad could track us with technology, I was less on board with googling anything even remotely connected to Crescent Moon Bearers, but books could be interesting. Embry and Gabriel hadn't communicated their plans with me, but they were both gone when Eric came by this morning. "I guess an hour couldn't hurt."

"It's very small. And boring. I would give it thirty minutes, tops."

I rolled my eyes then shook my head at him. He had no idea how long I could spend in a library.

· · ·

WE LEFT a note in case the guys came back, and took the horses so we could pretend we stumbled on the library and couldn't resist, rather than admit that we planned on defying the rules they put in place to keep me safe. We left the horses tied to the well and walked less than five minutes through the woods before we got to a road made of gravel, which told me people didn't often come this way.

I hesitated before stepping past the point that clearly represented the edge of the property, then quickly crossed the road to get to the library. Eric was right about it being tiny. I was surprised it was even open, with an actual employee sitting behind the desk to welcome us.

"Oh, hi," she said, looking up from her screen four times before acknowledging us.

"Hi." I looked for a computer or some other index system we could use to find what we were looking for.

"I'm so sorry, you're the first...how can I help you? What are you looking for?" She sprung to her feet, knocking over the plate of samosas she'd been enjoying while playing what sounded like pinball.

"Oh, don't worry about that. Is there an index?"

"We replaced all the shelves last summer, so I can tell you where absolutely everything is," she assured me.

"Two things, completely unrelated, but umm...We have a school project on witchcraft and prophecies, then I also want to look into Elizabeth Owens. She lived next to his grandfather's place, a long time ago, so if you had some kind of records..."

"Say no more." She beamed with excitement. "I'll be right back."

"Witchcraft and prophecies?" Eric asked while the librarian ran off through the shelves.

"I have many interests," I dismissed it.

"For what it's worth, I didn't believe grandpa until you made the balls of fire float," he shared, letting me know he wasn't oblivious.

"It was a ball of paper that I set on fire."

"But you're not denying it?" He cocked his head.

"Would you believe me if I did?"

"No," he admitted. "But I could pretend if it makes you feel better."

"I would pretend too if I could convince myself."

"Not a fan?" He furrowed his brow.

"It's very new," I tried to explain my reluctance without eliciting the pity I had mostly avoided thus far. "There have been a lot of new things in my life lately, and none of them are good."

"None of them?" he teased, giving me an out.

"Maybe one or two of them," I conceded.

"Much better." He smiled as the girl came back with a pile of books.

"This is the key to the micro-fiche rooms if you want to know about anything that happened in New Orleans in the past few centuries. We should have all the newspapers available." She handed us a key and pointed to a room in the corner. "And these are the best books on the occult that we have. I mean, we have the standards, but these are more...obscure," she told me, but I had no idea what the standards were. "I'm Jessica if you need anything."

"Thank you."

ERIC CARRIED the books to a secluded table in the empty library and handed me one.

"What did she mean by the standards?" he asked, flipping through the pages. He clearly wasn't enjoying whatever he saw in them.

"I have no idea. It's all new to me," I reminded him.

"What are we looking for?"

"Anything that mentions the Bearer of the Crescent Moon." I flipped to the index.

"Sounds fancy."

"Believe me, it's not."

The first book I opened was on magic through the ages. The 'obscure' part of it was a section on spells in the back, which included pictures of their effects, that turned my stomach more than anything. Eric's book was really cool, on witchcraft in New Orleans. I made a mental note to ask Ingrid about it, because I could swear one of the pictures was her.

"What was that?" I stopped Eric as he flipped through a volume on the Salem Witch Trials.

"Inquisition Scandals." He flipped back a few pages and summarized it for me. "There's a judge who sent his cousin's wife to burn at the stake, instead of the simple hanging all the other witches were sentenced to. His great-great-grandson also wrote a book they consider shameful."

I saw the picture and something clicked in my mind; Hathorne was the name of the judge at the Salem Witch Trials. He was the only one who never repented, but I had read the name in the Chronicles as well. I barely had time to grab the book before I was gone…

I WAS ANNABELLE, walking through Henry's property. She was familiar with it, practically showing Henry the way to a gazebo that overlooked a creek. She thought of it as her gazebo now. He'd told her that no one ever used it, but since she admitted how much she loved the view, he made it a staple of their walks. She pointed out the fresh coat of paint he added to the old wood, but every time they came, something was done to make the place more beautiful and inviting, be it clearing the dead leaves or putting out a vase of fresh flowers.

"I have a surprise for you," Henry said once we were seated. There

was a small wicker table between us, upon which there was a candle, some paper, and an inkpot.

"Are you writing me a letter?" Annabelle teased.

"I am actually going to show you a part of me I keep hidden. A secret of sorts, that I believe it is time I trust you with." He was still smiling, so she felt no fear, only curiosity.

First, he dipped his quill in the inkpot, then used his right hand to shield his words from her gaze as he wrote on the paper. She straightened up, ready to read it, but he carefully folded the paper, then put the tip over the candle, until it caught flame. A trick I knew well.

"Why did you do that? How can I read it now?" she playfully reproached, trying to reach for it to put out the flames, but he pulled it away and let go. At first, she was worried it would burn his trousers as it fell, but the paper did not fall. The flames spread so the entire paper was ablaze, then he waved his hands and it floated to her, landing on our side of the wicker table. She reached forward to put it out, but was amazed when she blinked and the paper was whole again, not a mark on it. As if there had never been a flame at all. Her introduction to magic was a lot less traumatizing than mine was.

"How did you do it?" she asked, searching the paper and the candle, looking around to see what could have done the trick.

"Magic." He winked. "Read it."

She raised her eyebrows, hoping to discover his secrets, before doing as she was told.

Will You Marry Me?

"Henry, I..." I could feel her struggle as she wanted to turn him down, but didn't want to hurt him. There really wasn't an appropriate way to tell him she was still in love with someone else.

"What are you afraid of?" He wasn't upset, he was kind. I could tell that he loved her. "Let me love you. Let me take care of you. Be my wife," he proposed.

Annabelle knew Henry would be a great husband, a good father, and he would make her happy. But then, part of the problem was that she wasn't sure if she deserved happiness anymore. I wanted to hold her in my arms and tell her everyone deserves love and happiness, but I knew I struggled with the same concerns these days. Henry was waiting for her answer, so she took another piece of paper from the pile, wrote "Maybe someday?", then folded it up and set it on fire as he had.

"What are you doing?" he asked, shaking his head with affection at her ignorance.

"That paper has my answer," she said, putting her concentration into moving the paper, excited more than anything when it also floated instead of falling onto the table. I understood what Embry meant when he said you just had to will it to happen.

"What's wrong?" she asked, still enjoying the trick, but Henry's eyes widened, and his brow furrowed.

"That isn't supposed to happen," he admitted, watching the flaming paper float between us.

"Of course not. It's magic." Annabelle smiled, oblivious to what was wrong. Eventually, she saw Henry was truly concerned, and reached for his hand. As she did, the paper landed in his lap, but he had to wave his hand so it wouldn't burn him. He read her answer and looked up, but his smile did not reassure her.

"You wanted me to say no?" she asked, confused by his reaction.

"No," he admitted, shaking his head as if to clear his thoughts. "I know I'll have to ask a few times before you get there. But that wasn't a trick."

"Of course, it was, Henry. You can't light a paper on fire then have it come back as good as new. You also can't make things fly," she reasoned.

"You're right, normal people can't."

"But we just did."

"My mother came from a long line of witches. When she had a son

instead of a daughter, she decided to teach me some of her magic. That is why I can do that with the paper and the fire."

"You can't be magic, Henry. I did the same thing. It's the paper. Or you did something to the fire."

"Or you're a witch." He was worried about her reaction, she could tell, but she also couldn't believe his story. She thought he was confused.

They spent the rest of the afternoon with him giving her little exercises, small magical acts that she had more and more trouble convincing herself were parlor tricks. It reminded me of that first week we tried spells to see what I could do. Henry was throwing challenges at Annabelle to convince her, but he was also impressed by her.

"So, I have magic?" Annabelle asked when she could no longer deny what he was showing her.

"You're very gifted," he agreed.

"And you would still wish to marry me?" Her mind went straight to Gabriel, and whether he and Embry would still love her, or be afraid of her now.

"More than anything in the world." Henry kissed her temple before leading her back to his house...

"Are you okay?" Eric asked me. He and Jessica were both standing over me, looking terrified.

"I'm fine." I tried to stand, but they wouldn't let me.

"Lucy," Eric argued, not believing me.

"I can call an ambulance," Jessica offered.

"No!" I cut her off mid-sentence. "I think I got too hot, and I skipped breakfast this morning…" I looked to Eric, pleading for him to get me out of it.

"It's okay, I'll bring her to the clinic." He gave me a look that said he was actually taking me there.

"Are you sure?"

"I am. Thank you so much for your help. I'll try to come

back next week." I smiled at her before getting up off the floor and letting Eric bring me outside.

IGNORING MY PROTESTS, he kept an arm around me to cross the street, into the woods.

"I'm fine, Eric, I promise," I told him.

"You're not fine," he argued. "You were, but then you saw something in the book and before you got a chance to freak out, you were on the floor. I am bringing you to a doctor or to Embry or something."

"You can't." A doctor would ask too many questions and I couldn't have him telling the guys that I willingly went off the property. That something happened while I was out, vulnerable and exposed. "It was just a memory."

"What does that mean?" Confusion replaced his concern.

"I sometimes get memories from my ancestors. One of them knew the guy in the book, Henry, so when I saw him…"

"You went into her memory of him?" he asked, looking at me like it made no sense, but also like he believed it.

"Sometimes I pass out when it happens, but other times I act it out, which led to me almost jumping off a barn." I looked up to him and smiled, to show him I really was okay, but I didn't look where I was going. I tripped on a tree root and instinctively shot my hands up to protect myself, but Eric's instincts were quick, and he reached out to catch me. Before I knew what happened, a burst of light shot out of my hands, knocking Eric into the side of the well.

"Eric!" I yelled in horror, rushing over to him. "Please don't be dead," I repeated to myself, shaking his limp and lifeless body.

CHAPTER FIFTEEN

"Eric! Oh my God, please wake up, please!"

I could hardly see through all my tears, but I felt his neck to make sure he had a pulse. He was still breathing, so CPR wouldn't help, but I needed something to do other than wait for him to be okay.

After what felt like hours, Eric stirred, garnering him all my attention. I moved the golden curls off his forehead for what must have been the hundredth time in the past few minutes, not sure what else to do.

He opened his eyes and looked around, disoriented and confused, but alive.

"Are you okay?" I asked, keeping my hand on his shoulder so he wouldn't stand up too quickly.

"I'm fine," he said, still trying to get his bearings.

"I'm so sorry. I didn't mean to… I would never want to hurt you."

"I know."

"This is what I was talking about. I can't control it and people get hurt and I am so sorry." The tears were warm as they ran down my cheeks, softening Eric.

"You have nothing to apologize for." His eyes finally focused on me.

"I thought you were dead." The sobs shook me as the adrenaline lost its purpose.

"I'm right here. I'm fine. It was my fault." He took me into his arms.

"I nearly killed you." I moved back so I could see his face, but stayed close enough that his arms were still around me. "I'm a death magnet. Everyone I care about dies." My breathing was back to normal, so I wasn't sobbing anymore, but the tears kept falling.

"I don't even have a scratch on me," he lied. There was no way landing on the wall of the well didn't do any damage, but he looked more worried about me than himself.

"I'll bring you back to Charlie's, then I'll stay away," I decided.

"You don't have to leave." He took my hand in his. I looked to him, so grateful for what he was trying to do, but I couldn't forgive myself if it happened again.

"Let's get you home." I gave him what I hoped was a reassuring smile, then helped him stand.

We each took our own horse, but it was like they knew something was up. They stayed close together, so I convinced myself I could catch him if he fell.

Eric stayed quiet until we arrived at the stables. He got off his horse and looked at me with the same concern I was looking at him with, only he didn't have my guilt.

"Can we talk about this, or were you planning on pretending nothing happened?" His look gave me the impression Option Two wouldn't be happening.

"You can ask," I said quietly. "But are you sure you're okay? Maybe we should take you to a clinic, just to be safe?"

"I've had way worse. I'm tougher than I look." He gave me a sad smile.

"I slammed you into a stone wall. With supernatural force," I reminded him.

"I touched you without asking." He shrugged.

"To stop me from falling flat on my face." I looked at him like he was insane to compare the two.

"You're more beat up about it than I am," he pointed out.

"I never meant to hurt you. To hurt anyone. It scares me," I explained. Even Annabelle's enthusiasm for the magic died when she realized it was real.

"Do you want to start at the beginning?"

"My beginning was normal." I never thought I would look back fondly on the days when I was just a little girl whose family kept dying around her.

"Until?" he pressed.

"Prom," I said simply before telling him how I escaped from the window and ran into Gabriel, who whisked me off to the plantation after admitting he promised my ancestor to protect her line until she returned. How he couldn't die until that happened. I told Eric how the bad guys found us, so we fled, visiting other Gifted. But the bad guys kept finding us. I struggled to tell him about the motel, how I have a birthmark the Big Bad is after, so he gave me the option of going willingly, but I didn't. I chose to fight instead, so Sam fought with me, and he died. They still got me and took me across the country with them until I escaped by killing someone and the guys found me.

"They said it would be over then, at least for a bit, but it wasn't. This lady found me in the washroom, and she was coming at me, but when I put out my hands, as if they could protect me...she disappeared."

"Into thin air?" Eric asked, having been amazingly quiet throughout my entire tale.

"She was gone, but there was a pile of ash on the floor. We

realized they found us with a tracker they put in Gabriel, so Embry took it out and we came here, where the guys decided I had magical powers and now they're trying to train me, so the Big Bad won't get me." I waited for his reaction, but he was taking his time, considering everything I'd shared.

"I guess I'm glad you only threw me into a wall and didn't turn me to dust."

I looked to him, horrified, but he was smiling.

"This isn't funny," I warned.

"I know, but I would rather see you laugh about it than cry."

"What kind of person would that make me?"

"One who made a mistake, because she can't control a new gift she never asked for, but who would never hurt a soul otherwise."

"A gift?"

"What kid doesn't wish for superpowers?" was his defense.

"It's not all it's cracked up to be."

"But it could be." He shrugged. "You could figure out how to use them and become a superhero. Teleport places. Fly," he gave options.

"I don't think it works like that," I argued, but he succeeded in making me smile.

It started to rain, so he took my hand as we ran to Charlie's, not stopping until we had shelter.

"What time do you leave tomorrow?" I asked him.

"Early." I could tell there was something he wanted to say, but I wasn't ready for him to make me feel better.

"Take care Eric." I gave him a goodbye hug, letting it last longer than I had intended, before leaving him standing there.

I WALKED in the direction of the villa, but I was overwhelmed by everything that happened in the past few months. I wanted to run, I wanted to punch things, I wanted to cry…I settled for a run through the trails in the rain, so I couldn't even tell if I was crying anymore. My legs burned and my shoes were soaked through, but I kept going until I had nothing left.

I WALKED BACK from the stables, taking a detour on the way to the villa so I could check in on Eric, maybe see him through the windows. I was walking around to the back patio when Charlie nearly made me jump out of my skin.

"Eric went to bed early. He has a lunch thing at school tomorrow." Charlie was sitting on a patio chair.

"He told you?" I asked, walking over. He looked concerned, but not afraid of me, so Eric mustn't have told him everything.

"Enough," he agreed. "How are you sweetie?"

"I just want to make sure Eric is okay."

"I'm making some tea; would you like some?"

"I'm good," I said, looking over to the villa. It was getting dark out, so the guys were either still out and I should be worried, or I was in trouble.

"Eric thought you might need some time." He caught my look.

"They know too?" I cringed.

"They were worried when you didn't come back, but Eric was home, the horses were in the stables…"

"I should head over."

"He'll be fine," he assured me. I just wasn't sure I would.

CHAPTER SIXTEEN

Apparently, spending the evening in the same room waiting for me did not mean that Embry and Gabriel had resolved any of their issues. Rather, the fact that they weren't avoiding each other meant they were finally letting it all out without holding back, calling each other on all their pent-up anger from the past three centuries.

I heard their raised voices as soon as I walked through the door. I found them in the living room and tried to cut in to get them to stop arguing, but as soon as I touched them, I was gone. Only it wasn't an Owens memory...

"It really is like losing Annabelle all over again, isn't it?" Embry asked while he and Gabriel sat at Rosie's bedside. It was the middle of the night, but she didn't look like she would make it to morning. She was pale and sweaty, every breath sounding like a losing battle. I was able to walk around the room, rather than being confined to whoever's memory this was.

Gabriel was anything but friendly, practically glaring at Embry.

"She isn't Annabelle," he argued. "She has her face, but she isn't her." Gabriel cringed, looking to my ancestor like he regretted his words. He and Embry both looked absolutely torn up by her imminent death.

"I'm sorry." Embry looked broken and apologetic. "Do you think there will be another?" he asked.

"There will never be another Annabelle," Gabriel argued.

"I know, but do you think there will be another one like Rosie, who looks like her?" Embry rephrased his question.

"You want one who loves you next time?" Gabriel was harsher than necessary. I remembered the look on his face when he told Rosie he didn't feel the same.

"Annabelle said she would come back," Embry reminded him.

"She said a lot of things," Gabriel turned him down, but whether they admitted it or not, they were both still waiting for her, even in my time...

"It's not like that for me. I love her like a daughter," Embry was saying when I woke up with both of them huddled over me. Someone had carried me into the living room and put me down on the couch.

"You did not love Annabelle, or any of the others, like a daughter. You were looking for your—" Gabriel called him on what he saw as a blatant lie.

"I was looking for Beth," Embry cut him off.

"You're awake." Gabriel noticed and helped me sit up.

"I'm fine," I assured them.

"What did you see?"

"Nothing useful," I tried to appear neutral.

"What happened this afternoon?" Gabriel brushed the hair out of my face. He was oblivious, but his attitude in the memory still stung.

"I tripped and accidentally knocked Eric into something," I

said dismissively, though it weighed heavy on my heart. I didn't want lectures on being more careful or needing more practice; I wanted them to make up for once and for all. "You should tell him," I told Embry.

"Tell me what?" Gabriel asked. He looked once to Embry, then tried to read my face.

"I didn't just stay here to help Beth with Helen after David died. Maybe at first, but...we were married," Embry admitted.

"You got your own." The words were meant to cut Embry, but as it was, they caused a pang in my chest.

"No, it had nothing to do with that. I understand what you meant, all those years ago...we had a son," he shared.

"A child?" Gabriel's mouth dropped.

"I got my happily ever after, Gabe. It ended, but I am not looking to replace her. I love Lucy like a daughter because she is the daughter of my daughter's daughter's daughter. As far as I'm concerned," he added, since Helen wasn't biologically his. "I'm not looking for anyone else. I'm ready to get up there so I can be with Beth again."

"You had a child and never told me about it?" Gabriel looked hurt.

"It was the first thing I wanted to do." Embry mirrored Gabriel's pain. "It seemed so wrong to not have you there, for you to not be Uncle Gabe...but we haven't been friends since I broke both your hearts."

"Both?"

"I know she loved you. I would never have done anything to take her from you, but you died, and she didn't deserve to be alone. She deserved someone who would love her and still be okay with her being in love with you. When you came back, yes, it hurt that I was going to lose her, but I knew that was the only way things could go. You two were meant to be, and I was the placeholder. Annabelle left, but if she had stayed, I would have been happy to step aside and let you both have your happily ever after."

"You weren't just holding my place," Gabriel argued, but the fight was out of him.

"Of course not. I loved Annabelle, and I would have fought any other man to have her, but not you. You were my best friend, you loved her first and...as much as I do believe she loved me; she could never love anyone the way she loved you. I am so sorry."

"Me too," Gabriel admitted.

They stood there, looking at each other for what felt like forever before they finally pulled each other in for a hug. They slapped each other on the back, as guys do, but I think it was the first hug in centuries for the two best friends who finally forgave each other.

I didn't dare interrupt, but after a while, they pulled apart and Gabriel asked, "You said a son?" looking like he knew exactly what that meant.

"I was lucky." Embry gave a sad smile.

"I'm sorry I never got to meet him."

"Me too."

"How were you lucky?" I hoped their son was an exception to Caleb's rule, and we had another branch to our family tree.

"Jack was with us for nineteen wonderful years."

I knew from the cemetery at the plantation that sons didn't make it past childhood. I think ten had been the oldest one I found.

"I'm sorry," I said. Jack was barely older than me.

"Don't be," Embry assured me. "We never thought we could get pregnant, so that in itself was a miracle. When we knew it was a boy, we assumed we would have a couple of years with him, tops. I got to see him grow up and find his passion."

"Was he a World War Two pilot?" Gabriel asked suddenly.

"A decorated war hero," Embry agreed with pride, the tears filling his eyes.

"I visited Helen not long after he died. She was torn up, but so vague about who he was to her."

"She doted on him like it was no one's business," Embry said fondly.

"What was he like?" I got the impression that after all this time keeping him a secret, Embry wanted to share.

"You don't need to humor me."

"I would love to get to know Jack," I assured him.

Embry went up to one of the two rooms he told us to ignore and came out with a large box full of letters, pictures, and rolls of film. When I mentioned that I would love to know about Helen too, he got another box, and we spent the rest of the night visiting Embry's past. There were a lot of tears, but also lots of smiles and happy memories about Embry's kids, then about my other ancestors and their kids...all the people Embry and Gabriel got close to, and then lost.

WE ORDERED pizza around ten o'clock, which I don't think I have ever done with them, and ate it in the living room while watching old home videos. One showed a visit from Gabriel, before Jack was born, so one minute we would see Gabriel entertaining Helen, then we would see Embry and Beth stealing a kiss in the background.

"I didn't want to upset you, or have you think I was using her, and she didn't want you to hate her for loving me," Embry responded to the question Gabriel wasn't asking.

"I think I see why Terrence called us stubborn idiots."

AFTER A WHILE, they took out some top-shelf bourbon, so I

decided it was time for me to get some sleep. I had spent most of the prior night tossing and turning.

We exchanged goodnights before I went to put my plate away. I lingered in the doorway, watching them laugh and catch up like the old friends I always wanted them to be. Gabriel must have felt me watching because he turned around and we locked eyes before I quickly headed upstairs. Not for the first time this summer, I wished I looked like anyone else.

CHAPTER SEVENTEEN

I was up long before Embry came downstairs the next morning. He looked like he spent the night partying, but happier than I had seen him other than in the memory with Beth.

"Sleeping in this morning?" I called him on it, cradling my cup of tea. I finished the Chronicles, which was more anti-climactic than anything. Unlike regular books, this one didn't have an ending. It went from a homemade remedy for chickenpox to a note saying another Bearer of the Crescent Moon was born on September 20th, 1990 to Marilyn Owens and Unknown. There were the shortest of entries marking occasions such as the first time the guys met me, when Mrs. Boyd died and Mr. Boyd insisted on raising me, then again when Mr. Boyd passed away and Sam refused to let them take me. It brought a tightness in my chest I wasn't expecting. When people asked, they always apologized for the loss of my mom, but no one really dwelled on the Boyds. For all intents and purposes, they were the ones who raised me until Sam took over, at which point he was more like a brother taking care of me than a parent.

It was different for Mrs. Boyd, because I had known my mom, albeit briefly, and Grams. She was always an additional motherly figure for me, but Mr. Boyd was the only father figure I ever had. *Unknown* never showed up, so every Father's Day, Mr. Boyd was the one who received my macaroni flowers and glitter cards. When he died, Sam and I would get together amid celebrating Sam's Father's Day to celebrate the man who raised us. He was everything you needed a father to be.

"Where's Gabriel?" Embry asked after pouring himself a cup of the coffee I brewed for them hours ago.

"He hasn't come down."

"He's not upstairs," Embry argued.

A fear came over me before I reminded myself of all the places he could be other than dead or captured.

"Morning." Gabriel came in after I mentally listed all his potential early morning escapes. Jogging, surveillance, training…

"How are you standing?" Embry asked.

"I switched to coffee after the third shot," Gabriel reminded him.

"How did you manage to sleep?" I chipped in.

"*That* is why I already did my 10k, showered, got attacked by a dog, and figured out a game plan for today."

"Attacked by a dog?" I asked while Embry inquired, "Game plan?"

"We disagreed over who should eat my last piece of bacon. He won," Gabriel told me. "And I went through the Shadow Book to see what we could work on today," he elaborated on the game plan.

I didn't bother telling him it was a Book of Shadows, as I'm pretty sure he does it on purpose. "I'm not doing magic anymore," I reminded him instead.

"We don't have to work on new stuff. We can use the burning paper thing," he tried.

"No." I shook my head, the image of Eric on the ground all the deterrent I needed.

"Or the floating spell. We can use any of the simple ones."

"I said no," I repeated, not quite storming off, but choosing that moment to get a refill on my tea.

I could hear them whispering about me before Gabriel came over to the kitchen, with Embry hanging back.

"I know your powers scare you, and you don't want to use them," he began.

"I don't," I agreed.

"But not using the powers intentionally doesn't mean you won't use them accidentally." He paused so I could remember what happened to Eric, but he was using it as motivation to learn. "If ever someone invades your personal space, creeps up on you, or—"

"I get the picture." Even catching me so I wouldn't fall could be deadly.

"I'm not blaming you, Luce, I'm saying it's new and you can't control it. Yet."

"When I try, people get hurt," I pointed out.

"That's why I thought we could work on that today."

"Using it wasn't helping," I argued.

"We're not going to learn new spells or practice the old ones for the sake of it. I want you to work on actively controlling your magic."

"How?" They kept saying I needed to control it, but never showed me the way, or anything that worked.

"Working on precision rather than power. Flinging your arms without making things happen. I want you to know how to not use them as well as how to master them."

"That sounds great in theory, but I'm not comfortable with any magic right now. I have nightmares of when I threw you into the tree, and Eric into the well, or when that woman..." I shuddered, remembering it, but I didn't want to say out loud that I killed her. "I feel evil when I use it."

"Magic is not inherently good or bad," Embry told me. "It all depends on how you use it. Good people can use it for bad things, bad people can use it for good things…"

"It's safer if I don't use it," I finished for him.

"If Clara creeps into your room next year on Christmas morning and jumps on your bed…" Gabriel asked me.

"That's not…why would you…" I could see it, because it was what Clara did every year.

"I don't want to scare you. I want to prepare you, so you never get that look on your face again," Gabriel explained, but he didn't apologize for going there.

"The more I use it…"

"I will never make you use it if you don't want to, but I think it's important for you to learn how to not use it when you don't want to."

I looked to both of them, terrified of what could happen from using my powers, but even more afraid of what could happen when I didn't mean to use them. "Okay," I reluctantly agreed.

EMBRY MADE US OMELETS, then we headed out to the field with the blanket, a stack of paper, a bag of rice, and a pouch of sand.

"How does this work?" I sat across from the guys with the random objects between us.

"We'll use rice first," Gabriel explained, pouring some out into a little pile in front of him. "I want you to make that one float without any of the others."

"Which one?" There were at least a half-dozen he could be pointing to.

"This one right here." He used a strand of wheat to point to a grain of rice under other grains.

"But not the others?" I verified.

"Exactly."

I took a breath, then got to work. The hardest part was keeping track of which grain I was targeting, but I got it on my first try.

"Impressive," Embry told me.

"Do you think you could lift these three, then lift that one up to here?" Gabriel asked again.

It was easy to get the three grains up, but harder to keep them in place while lifting the other one higher. They faltered the first few times, but eventually, I got them to remain stable while the other one came higher.

"I thought rice might be beneath you." Gabriel scooped up the remaining rice and put it back into the bag.

"Sand?" I asked as he spread it out between us.

"Precision helps with control," he explained.

"What am I doing with the sand?" I sighed, but he was right. I was focusing harder and learning how to single elements out. My magic would be better if I chose to use it now, but I didn't see how this helped me not use it by accident.

"I'm not going to point at a grain in particular, but I want you to lift one."

"Just one?"

"I might not entirely understand all the intricacies of your powers, but so far you seem to need to concentrate and visualize what you're working on…"

"But this is just a pile of sand," I understood.

My first attempt lifted at least a pinch of sand, as did my second and third.

"Try pulling one from this." Gabriel scooped a bit of sand into his palm, sensing my exasperation.

"Isn't that cheating?"

"We'll come back to the pile," he assured me.

Every time I lifted a few, he took them in his hand, then

dropped the excess when I levitated some. This went on until I had a single grain of sand floating between us.

"Again," Gabriel encouraged, but he stopped dropping the excess, so I had to play with the pinch of sand in his hand until I got it down to one.

Once I got that consistently, we tried with the big pile again. After two tries, I levitated a single grain every time.

"Should I separate atoms now?" I asked, taking a sip of the iced tea Embry brought us.

"Now we play with paper." Gabriel smiled.

"Play?" I asked.

"You know how the paper catches fire, you float it to me, then the fire disappears?"

"We spent the afternoon passing notes," I agreed.

"This time, don't let it burn."

"Protect the paper?" I was confused. Being the one who set the fire meant if I didn't want it to burn, I just had to not set it on fire.

"No, start burning it, but keep it contained. Don't let the entire thing be consumed."

"Do I still float it to you?"

"If you can." He smiled, making it a challenge.

It turned out that floating the paper to him was the least of my problems. Unlike the rice and sand, I didn't have to isolate a grain. I had to set the paper on fire, then control the flames that were moving of their own accord. I had to prevent them from engulfing the rest of the paper, which was what they tried to do.

It took me at least a dozen tries, with varying amounts of scorchedness, before I finally passed.

CHAPTER EIGHTEEN

"I get that I can be more precise when I use my powers now, but I don't know how that stops me from hurting people," I asked after another morning spent working on the minutiae of simple spells. I appreciated that the magic was focused on objects for now, but I didn't know how long that would last.

"You don't feel like you have more control over what you're doing?" Embry asked, waving to someone in the distance.

"I was told you needed living targets you wouldn't feel bad for hurting." Ingrid walked over, wiggling her fingers at me.

"I thought the goal was to not hurt people?" I argued.

"To not hurt them accidentally," Embry agreed. "But we don't want you to be afraid to use your powers on real threats."

"Why are you so bent on making me use my powers when your plan is to keep me as far away from everything as possible?"

"Since you insist on not running next time they find us…" Embry paused, waiting for me to change my mind, but I didn't. "Our plan is to keep you as far away from the danger, and die protecting you."

"That's not a plan, that's suicide," I argued.

"We're not opposed to you helping out mystically from the shadows," Gabriel relented.

"You want me to hide away from the danger and what? Will them all to explode?" I asked. "If that's something I'm capable of, shouldn't I do it now, from here? Wouldn't Beth and Annabelle have tried if it was that easy?"

"We don't know what you can do, Luce. We can tell that you're powerful and not the damsel in distress one would assume you are…"

"But we won't know anything if you refuse to try," Embry finished for him.

"Do you have a Big Bad for me to practice on?" They were being ridiculous.

"I do." Ingrid shrugged conspiratorially.

"It's…you don't know what he can do. You don't know how he would retaliate, or…"

"We can at least see what you could do to his army," Embry suggested.

"We can try." I sighed, not really wanting to do this.

INGRID WAITED for me to say I was ready, then closed her eyes. For a moment, everything was calm and quiet, but then a huge black cape jumped out at me from nowhere. I instinctively put my arms up to protect myself, and the hooded figure burst into nothingness.

"Very cool," Ingrid told me.

"Not when it's a person," I argued. Maybe it wouldn't bother me so much if blowing it up had been my intention, rather than completely unintentional.

"Do you want to try again?" Gabriel offered. I didn't think practice would help, but I didn't know what else to do to not accidentally hurt people I cared about.

"Can they look more like people?" I braced myself.

"Of course." Ingrid gave me a knowing smile.

Even though I knew what was coming, I still blew up the first three illusions she attacked me with. They definitely looked human, but also large and intimidating, brandishing weapons so I would recognize them as threats. I eventually managed to stop exploding them, but I still sent them flying in a way no human would survive.

"How about we take a quick break?" Embry suggested.

"Maybe if I exhaust myself the powers will go away?" I asked hopefully.

"If you're anything like Beth, I'll burn out before you do," Ingrid told me. "And I don't burn out."

"I'm trying to concentrate, but they come at me, and my head goes blank," I lamented.

"Maybe think of the force shield?" Gabriel suggested.

"That still hurts people."

"Then let's go again." Ingrid sent illusions my way without waiting for me to be ready.

Again, I blew up a number of them, then produced a shield they bounced off of at an alarming speed, before one finally froze less than a foot away from me.

"That's awesome," Embry praised once Ingrid paused the attacks.

"Think you can do that again?" she asked me.

"I can try." I took a deep breath and got to work.

For the rest of the afternoon, I successfully froze every hooded and menacing figure Ingrid threw at me.

"Maybe I can do it because my subconscious knows I'm not really in danger," I ventured.

"Not in danger?" Ingrid asked.

"You're sending illusions at me."

"Very powerful ones." She was offended.

"They're scary, but they're holograms." I didn't want to be mean, but I wasn't at risk for a heart attack, and that was the most damage they could do to me.

"I beg to differ." She conjured one and made it run into a bushel of hay, that exploded from the impact.

"That's what would have happened to me if I succeeded in putting my hands up and doing nothing?" I questioned her sanity.

"I get that you don't want to blow up an innocent kid who spooks you on Halloween, but the idea is also to not let you die if a scary person literally throws himself at you," she said, shrugging her shoulders.

"I didn't know they were real." Gabriel put his hand out to stop me from reproaching him. "But she is right as far as our goals."

"Unless they destroy my heart with the impact," I ventured.

"Your heart is remaining intact." Gabriel pointed a finger at me.

"Every heart breaks at some point."

"I'll break the boy or girl who does that to you." Embry winked at me.

We went again with me knowing the threat was real, even if it was in my imagination, and I managed to freeze anyone that came between my hands.

When it got dark, Embry accompanied Ingrid to her car while Gabriel walked back to the villa with me.

"Dying won't bring him back," Gabriel said delicately as I rolled the band Clara gave me through my fingers.

"I know that." I slipped it back on. Embry was usually the one who called me out on bad thoughts.

"I mean it, Lucy. If the Big Bad comes for you and you do nothing…forget the fact that we've been protecting your family for over three hundred years…your death is the absolute worst-case scenario that makes everything else no longer worthwhile. Them getting your heart would mean the end of the world, but we have never once considered destroying it beforehand to prevent that."

"Maybe you should."

"Lucy." There was venom in his tone.

"If I had a nuclear bomb in my chest that was ready to go off at any moment, but killing me permanently deactivated it, I'm pretty sure every government would vote to neutralize me."

"But you're not a bomb. You're not a thing to be neutralized. You're a human being with hopes and dreams and a heart of gold who deserves to share it with the world, not hide it." He let the words sink in.

Tears stung my eyes, so I brought my hand to my temple and tried to shake it off. "Aren't you tired?" I asked him quietly. I had been running for a few months, but this was what his life looked like for the past few hundred years.

"If you die, we die, like we should have centuries ago. But I will spend every last breath I have making sure you get out of this and have your happily ever after."

"What difference do you really think I can make?"

"We'll never know if we don't try. But I believe you can do anything you set your mind to. Not just because you were a genius before this, but you have aced every obstacle the world has thrown at you."

"It was fake," I reminded him.

"The threats might be sometimes, but the magic isn't. I didn't know about Beth's powers, and Annabelle felt the same way you do about it, but I would imagine that if you let yourself be what you were born to be, you can do it all."

CHAPTER NINETEEN

On Sunday, the guys gave me a rest day as far as magic was concerned, so we worked on my self-defense. I was getting better at controlling what magic came out of me, but I still felt more comfortable with physical attacks. Much to the guys' dismay.

"Your jab needs work, but you've got a solid right hook." Gabriel gave me a smile while we walked back to the villa for lunch. It was an exhausting morning, but I loved almost every minute of it.

"Sweet tea?" Embry grabbed a pitcher from the fridge. I saw his eyes go wide as someone grabbed me from behind. I turned to see who it was, instinctively raising my arms in defense. I was paralyzed with fear, but it was a little girl standing in front of me. She looked confused and so innocent that I panicked before realizing that I didn't blow her up or send her into the wall behind her. Nothing happened.

"What the hell?" I asked when the girl disappeared. I was on high alert with my heart pounding out a marathon in my chest.

"It's okay, you're okay." Gabriel came over and took me in his arms.

"She would have turned into a rainbow if you'd done something, so you would know she was one of my holograms," Ingrid defended herself, rounding the corner.

"Am I broken?" I asked in reference to the fact that I braced my arms, and nothing happened.

"When you saw she was a kid, did you want to hurt her?" Gabriel asked.

"No, but that hasn't mattered any other time," I pointed out. Ingrid had slowly been making her illusions less threatening, but the best I could do was freeze them when they came at me.

"It isn't that you're broken. You were able to control your powers enough that they're triggered by you, not by your fear," Ingrid explained.

"You tricked me into nearly destroying Embry's kitchen…"

"To show you that you don't need to be afraid of your powers."

"One time."

"But you felt it," Ingrid called me on it. "You decided not to hurt her, so you didn't."

"Maybe warn me next time?" I asked of her, my heart slowly going back to normal.

"You don't always get warnings," she said simply. "And it would have put a damper on the party if we didn't give you a practice round."

"What party?" I asked before Charlie and Eric came out of the living room, holding up a handmade 'Happy 19th Birthday!' banner.

"For she's a jolly good fellow…" they started singing, reminding me of my graduation party as I realized today was my birthday.

"I completely forgot." I wasn't sure if I was more shocked that I forgot, or that they remembered.

"We thought you might." Embry came over and gave me a hug.

"There's so much else going on," I pointed out.

"There is," Gabriel agreed. "But you need to celebrate the small stuff."

I raised my eyebrows. That was not the advice I expected to hear from him of all people.

"You've been through a lot, and we don't want you to burn out," he downplayed it.

"Taking care of my mental health?"

"Reminding you that it's not just the fate of humanity you're fighting for. You yourself are worth saving," Embry told me.

"I have a shop to get back to, but I am leaving you this." Ingrid handed me a package wrapped with a shawl instead of wrapping paper.

"You really didn't have to," I argued. I was never good at accepting gifts.

"I wanted to," she assured me, putting her forehead against mine with a smile, before she headed off.

I removed the shawl to reveal a surprisingly modern book on the history of magic. I was expecting spells or a potion book to help me defeat the Big Bad, but reading the back cover revealed it was a study on where magic comes from, its limits, and its affinity for good or evil. Mental health was clearly the theme of the day.

"You came back for this?" I asked Eric, really happy to see him.

"Of course. It's your birthday." He smiled. "Come on." He took my hand and brought me to the living room, where balloons were on the floor, the walls, and floating in mid-air. There was also a table with a bunch of finger foods and a bowl of some purple-colored punch.

"You got me something?" I was surprised when he took out a box, roughly the size of a mini ruler.

"Made it," he corrected.

"Oh." I set my expectations to something with lots of glue

and construction paper, because that's what Clara usually gave me. Instead, I found a beautiful fountain pen. "You made this?" He didn't seem like the type to lie to impress me, but I had serious doubts.

"I maybe slightly exaggerated that statement. I found the pen and made adjustments."

"Adjustments?" I asked instead of confirming that 'found' meant he stole it from Charlie.

"Don't do it now, because you'll either pop a balloon or hurt someone, but when you twist off the cap and press this button on the end, you get one of these." He lifted a flap in the box to show me tiny, needle-like inserts.

"Poison?" I asked, wondering what kind of people I was hanging out with.

"A toxin," he corrected.

"The difference would be…"

"It's not a poison that kills people, it's a toxin that should knock them out for maybe an hour. Which is long enough for you to get away."

"And you made it for me?" I couldn't believe how sweet it was of him to offer me an alternative to killing or using magic.

"It's your birthday." He shrugged, but his eyes told me it had everything to do with me, and nothing to do with the date.

"I love it." I tried to be serious, but had to suppress a laugh. I never would have imagined myself being this touched by a pen that shoots tranquilizer darts.

"I'm glad." He smiled before his grandfather motioned me over to the couch.

"They're not new," Charlie warned, taking a big box from beside him. "But these will be a lot better than your hiking shoes."

"I can't take these." I had no idea how much riding boots cost, but these looked like they hadn't been used more than once or twice, and they were gorgeous.

"Of course you can. Some of my granddaughters are less into nature than others."

"Thank you," I told him, sensing 'no' wasn't an option. "Not just for the boots, but for everything you've done since I got here. For this." I looked around the villa, that he and Eric turned into a birthday explosion for me. I had completely missed Deanna's birthday back in July, and I wasn't sure if I wanted to be back in time for Clara's, or let her have one more year before finding out about Sam. I'm sure they had their doubts, but if I hadn't seen it happen, I would have convinced myself he somehow managed to get away.

"It's what you do for family," Charlie said, like it was nothing.

"I'm a stranger," I pointed out.

"You're anything but. For as long as I can remember, your family has been mine."

"You can never have too much family." I smiled instead of arguing.

"I've always believed you choose your family. Sometimes you're lucky enough to be born into it, but sometimes you have to fight for them." He shrugged at the last part.

"I'm very glad to have you as mine," I thanked him again, this time with a hug, before he guided me to the food table.

Charlie gave me a description of all my options and filled a plate of things for me to try. Then left to deal with an alarm in the kitchen, announcing more food.

"I'm sorry we couldn't bring you to them. Or them to you," Gabriel apologized when he found me holding the overstuffed plate, playing with my ring, and staring into space.

"I can't lose anyone else." I was good with keeping them as far away from me as possible.

I could see he wanted to say something, to remind me that none of this was my fault, that Sam knew what he was getting himself into… a million things that wouldn't make a difference. Instead, he took a tiny pouch from his pocket and handed it to me.

"Happy birthday," he said with a shy smile, which was intriguing more than anything. Embry was an expert at presents. He always got me exactly what I never knew I always wanted, from rare books to microscopes or online classes…it was always out of the box and always perfect. Gabriel, on the other hand, would give me something Deanna picked out and wrapped for him, a gift card, or nothing.

The way he watched me open it made me nervous, as I fumbled with the knot tied in the string.

"Wrapped it yourself?" I tried to lighten the mood.

"I think we all went a little homemade this year," he agreed.

"What is it?" There was a thin stone the size of my palm hanging from a delicate silver chain.

"A necklace." He smiled, getting me to roll my eyes.

"You know what I mean."

"It's moonstone," he shared, then continued when I failed to react to the name. "It's supposed to help you channel and control your energy. It also brings protection."

"You believe in that stuff?" I wasn't judging or making fun of him, but I was curious. He surprised me a lot this summer.

"I trust people who do, and I figure it can't hurt. Plus, being the Bearer of the Crescent Moon, if any rock was going to help you, it would have to be moonstone."

"That's a good point." I gave him a smile and took a closer look at the stone. It was beautiful, whether it protected me or not. It wasn't quite blue, but there was a bluish sheen to it. It had a smooth, oval-ish shape, but there were scratches on the back. I didn't want to point out the flaws of his defective stone, but I wondered if they would influence the stone's power. Then I realized the scratches were deliberate. "What's on the back?" I asked, staring at the stone in my hand to try and make it out.

"I tried something, but I'm not sure it turned out." He took the stone and held it up to the sunlight coming in from the window, with the scratches facing me.

"You did this?" I tried not to, but I could feel my eyes water. He somehow carved Sam, Clara, and Deanna into the back of the stone, so I could carry them with me always.

I didn't wait for his answer, I rushed forward and hugged him. I held him tight, waiting until the tears stopped and I'd wiped away the evidence before pulling back.

"Thank you." I looked into his eyes, but failed to convey how much I meant it.

"Of course." Gabriel looked at me in a way that gave me butterflies, like when Eric did, only my heart joined in, beating faster than it was supposed to.

"Would you mind?"

Without waiting for his answer, I pulled my hair to one side and offered him my back.

His hands were warm on my neck as they fumbled with the clasp, but they still sent shivers down my spine. I smiled at Embry when he looked over, hoping I wasn't as flushed as I felt.

"I'll let you enjoy your food and get back to your party." Gabriel gave me a smile.

I wanted to argue that he wasn't bothering me and could stay, but instead I let him go talk to Charlie, who seemed to have a million stories to tell him and Eric.

After a while, Embry suggested everyone get fresh air and sunlight, so the party moved outside.

"I don't think I can top everyone else," Embry apologized, taking a seat beside me in the yard.

"You have ten years on them," I assured him. "And no one had to get me anything. It completely slipped my mind."

"Because you feel like you don't deserve to celebrate, which is absolutely not the case." He waited for me to look over and acknowledge it, so I rolled my eyes at him.

"Remember this when your birthday comes around," I warned, but I hoped we wouldn't still be on the run come March.

"Oh, I expect cake, singing, and streamers," he teased.

"Your wish is my command." I smiled.

He smiled back before handing me a red leather photo album. There was only one picture per page, but as soon as I opened it, I knew the perfect-gift-giver struck again.

"It's perfect," I told him. There was something about pictures of my mother I had never seen before that made me feel like I was getting another piece of her.

"I put a few pictures of the Boyds near the end, for when you're homesick, but most of them are of her."

"Thank you." I flipped through the first pages. "Is that...."

"A much younger Charlie," he agreed. "And this one is Eric's father if I'm not mistaken."

"Six boys?" I asked, seeing a pattern of large families.

"Only five of them were Charlie's. This was where all the kids ended up every weekend. I only gave you the pictures with Marilyn."

"I appreciate that," I told him before spotting Gabriel across the pool, letting Eric use him for a demonstration in his story. It was surprisingly action-intensive for the smiles they were sharing. I definitely hadn't seen Gabriel smile this much, ever.

"It's okay to choose him," Embry brought me back to the conversation.

"Choose him for what?" I asked, surprised by how serious he looked.

"To love Gabriel," he said bluntly, his unwavering stare forcing me to be the one to look away.

"I love both of you." My eyes focused on a tiny spot in the corner of the photo album.

"Not the way you love him," he argued.

"I'm just trying to survive at the moment."

Embry looked at me like he didn't believe a word I was saying. The flushed cheeks from earlier probably weren't helping my case.

"Even if I did, it wouldn't matter, because he loves Annabelle and no one else. You should have seen how heartbroken Rosalind was when Gabriel turned her down." I remembered the memory from the train. "Beth was lucky she fell for you and got to have a bit of a happy ending."

"Luce…" Embry looked at me with…not pity, but possibly compassion, as if he knew what I was going through.

"There is absolutely nothing that says I have to fall for one of you. I can break the cycle like Cassie and fall madly in love with someone else. Like Eric, or a stranger who has no idea about any of it," I argued with his empathetic look.

"You definitely can," he agreed. "I'll be happy with whatever you choose, as long as it makes you happy."

"He loves Annabelle. Not the way she looks," I reminded him. I didn't want to get into it, but I had to shut him down.

"But he also loves you. Not because you're a Bearer who looks like her, but because you're you. And I was there when he said he saw you," he reminded me.

"And it broke his heart."

"I'm just saying it's okay if you choose him. You can do what you want with that, but I will love you forever, no matter what," he assured me before Eric motioned for us to come join them. I gave Embry a hand and we went back to the party, which lasted long after the sun went down.

CHAPTER TWENTY

I tried to clear my mind and focus. I held the moonstone in my hand and thought of why I was doing this. Why it mattered if I lived or died. I didn't want to die, of course, but no one wants to. I thought of Clara and Deanna, who didn't deserve to lose anyone else. Then I thought of Sam, knowing I was the reason they lost him. It filled me with guilt and made me think everyone would be better off if we destroyed my heart, and me along with it. But Sam would never forgive me. We were raised to be anything but selfish, or weak, which is what sacrificing myself would be. I would be taking the easy way out to let someone else be hunted. More importantly, if I died without defeating the Big Bad, or living a long and happy life, then Sam died for nothing. Even the guilt at causing his death wouldn't let me make his death be in vain.

I took a deep breath and nodded to let Ingrid know I was ready, opening my eyes just as her illusions came for me, one after the other. Some were dressed in black with swords and guns, a few looked like Clara, while most were more ambiguous.

Ingrid was right, that fear was usually the driving force behind any magic I did. This time I buried the fear and used intent, the element I made fun of when this all began. Instead of reacting out of fear, I evaluated what was coming for me, even anticipating them. I blasted the ones looking to hurt me, and froze the ones I wasn't sure about, time after time, until Ingrid suggested we take a break.

"I can keep going," I assured them, sweating as if I just ran a marathon.

"I can't," Ingrid argued. "You're destroying them faster than I can conjure new ones."

"I'm sorry." I took a seat beside her on the lawn chairs.

"Don't be," she assured me. "You're doing amazing."

"But we still don't know what his powers are actually like."

"We don't," Gabriel agreed. "But you can definitely take on his army."

"From behind us, preferably in a reinforced steel room that only your magic works in," Embry amended.

"I think I need to see them for it to work," I argued.

"We'll cross that bridge when we get there," they assured me.

WE TRIED it a few more times, with bigger, more powerful illusions rather than a constant flow of them. I was still feeling in control of myself and my powers, but the confidence was only slightly stronger than the fear.

"I would definitely not want to get on your bad side," Ingrid encouraged.

"You're going?" I asked when she grabbed her purse from the lawn chair.

"I left Mr. Fraser in charge of the shop, but I need to go close up and make sure he hasn't burned the place down. It's been busier with yet another disappearance last week."

"Someone you knew?" I asked.

"Only by look." She gave me a hug before going to see Charlie next door.

·   ·   ·

"How are you feeling?" Embry asked me.

"Okay," I said after considering it.

"Don't hate us too much?"

"Only a little bit," I was mostly joking.

"Are you both good if I bail on dinner and help Ingrid with something?" Embry asked.

"Of course," I assured him, while Gabriel nodded.

"It shouldn't take all night," Embry assured me before heading off.

"Have fun," I called after him, then turned to Gabriel, "I need to remove this magical exertion, but I can make pasta or something when I'm done?"

"I'll cook. You've done more than enough today." He gave me a smile before going to the kitchen as I headed for the stairs.

After my shower, I found a tight white tank top, then wrapped the shawl Ingrid gave me for my birthday around my waist, turning it into a skirt. I wanted to take advantage of our time in New Orleans, before we went back to chicken coops and tiny boats, which had to be coming soon. The shawl was a deep burgundy color that, paired with the moonstone necklace, made me feel like Esmeralda from the Halloween costume I wore when I was six or seven. The Boyds gave up on most of Grams' traditions, although I did convince Mrs. Boyd to make us all soul cakes before we went trick-or-treating around the block.

I came downstairs and found Gabriel at the stove, stirring what smelled like a pesto-parmesan sauce. Part of me had worried he would make up an excuse like 'securing the perimeter' to avoid me, while part of me wanted him to. Which might have something to do with Embry telling me it was okay to love him.

"Johnny Cash?" I asked of what sounded like a record from the scratchiness.

"Embry was storing the record player with the pots and pans, no idea why, but I haven't found any other records yet," he defended the selection.

"Can I help with anything?" I offered.

"You just sit, relax and read the Book of Shadows or something."

I WENT OVER and got Ingrid's book on magic. It was weird because it looked like the newly published, commercial witch stuff that was the trend of my elementary school days, but I couldn't see Ingrid giving me a capitalist account on magic, from people who had no idea whether or not it even existed.

I wasn't reading every page, definitely not as thoroughly as I should, but I was learning a lot about magical theory. Like how it travels but never dies, how some people can have it in them but be unable to do anything, while others can draw on the magic of people around them...apparently, those people can not only 'borrow' powers when they have none of their own, but go so far as to steal it if they do.

It was in the third chapter, called 'Other Magical Beings' that I found a section on 'The Gifted' that explained why Ingrid chose to give me this particular book. I almost skipped it, because it listed faeries, goblins, and other creatures that had no place in the real world, even if witches apparently did.

'Gifted are a subset of humans with supernatural abilities that manifest in their second lives, although there have been first life manifestations. Gifted stay alive, even in death, until a specific task – unique to them – has been completed.'

The book wasn't clear on the intricacies of coming back to life, but it did mention instances where the body was too far gone for the Gifted to come back, such as in nuclear explosions, being entirely dissolved in acid, and meticulous dismemberment.

Apparently, some Gifted never figure out what they were meant to do, especially the healers and first responders who rarely know which patient did the trick. Others, like Embry and Gabriel 'become Gifted by making a promise the fates decide they deserve to keep.'

A lot of it I already knew, but the book went into oddly specific details on some aspects. There was a list at the end of it, of 'Notable Historical Figures Rumored to be Gifted' which included Nostradamus, Leonardo da Vinci, Queen Victoria, Carl Jung, Adolf Hitler, and George Lucas. Each of them was said to have suffered terrible incidents, like car accidents, plagues, and assassination attempts no one thought they would survive before accomplishing incredible feats.

The most shocking to me was the part on scientific studies; 'Gifted become paranormal beings once they enter their second lives, so biological functions such as aging, menses and reproduction become impossible.' There were tables of scientific evidence to back it up, but I had Embry's word that disproved it.

"How's the book?" Gabriel asked me after covering a wok-style pan and putting something else in the oven.

"Part of it makes me think it was written to make money off suckers who want to believe in magic, but other parts make me wonder if the author wasn't a Gifted witch who saw it all happen."

"I don't think that's a good thing."

"It mentions that Gifted can't have kids." I thought about Terrence's daughter Angela, Embry's son...I knew many exceptions. "Is it only Gifted women, or is the book wrong?"

"The book is right. It causes a lot of heartbreaks. Etta was devastated when she found out."

"How do you explain Angela and Jackson?" I argued.

"Angela was born before Terrence died, and the twins were adopted," he reminded me. "And as far as Jackson...maybe your line is different."

"We can have kids with dead people?" I asked, instantly regretting it. "I don't mean it like that, but after you first die, your life is put on hold until you accomplish your purpose."

"It's a fair question," he assured me. "It might be because of the Prophecy. There also seems to be a lack of certainty involving Gifted. Some get to live out their lives when they finish their task, others fade away. Death sometimes gives you new powers, or takes old ones away...I really don't know." He got pensive.

"The book has a whole section on controlling your magic instead of letting it control you. I've only skimmed it so far, but they do suggest moonstone," I changed the subject for him.

"There's hope for me yet." He winked before a timer went off. He took cheesy garlic bread out of the oven, then went to scoop some pesto-parmesan tortellini onto two plates.

"It smells like an Italian restaurant." I breathed it all in and he watched me with a smile.

"I figured you just had your birthday, but you didn't get any pasta, so..."

"It's perfect," I assured him.

"How was it today?" he asked, bringing the plates to the table so we could eat.

"Which part?" I blew on my tortellini before tasting it. It would be wrong to say I could die happy now, but the sentiment was there.

"Did it tire you out, were you weakened by it... I guess all of it."

"It's weird." I tried to find a way to explain it. "When we stopped, I felt like I ran a marathon, as you could see," I referenced the sweaty mess I became. "But at the same time, it was like my body was used to running marathons and I could do more. It was sort of outside of me, but inside me at the same time."

"I guess it's like my speed," he mostly said to himself, taking a piece of the garlic bread.

"How does your speed work?"

"I run in the mornings, to stay healthy and clear my head, but eventually I need to stop, because my legs are on fire. I need to rest and eat and give it a day. If I'm not consistent, my legs will be sore for days when I get back into it."

"That's just regular running," I pointed out.

"I know. When I'm using my speed, it's the same muscles, and I'm using them more intensely, but I could keep going for as long as I need to, without getting tired, and my legs will be fine."

"That's really weird."

"The only time I can't sustain my speed like that is after I die, before it recovers completely."

"I guess this is a stupid question, but did you run away a lot as a kid?"

I got a smile as he finished his bite.

"My family was not wealthy, so if I wanted to impress others, I had to work twice as hard and get more done in the same time frame as everyone else. I was incredibly hard on myself and always pushed to be faster, so I could earn the respect others were born with."

"It wasn't about the running."

"Nope," he agreed. "I can't outrun a bullet, or flick it out of the way, but it is a bit like time slows down around me when I'm in it. I could write, swim, start an assembly line with it instead. The running just comes in handy."

"To save the damsel in distress."

"I believe you've more than proved that title inaccurate."

"Don't hand in your plate of armor just yet."

"I'll always be there for you Luce," he assured me.

"Until we defeat the Big Bad," I agreed. A shiver ran through me.

Gabriel smiled instead of telling me that was a pipe dream.

"This is delicious."

"I very briefly worked in a restaurant," he shared.

"Really?" I was very skeptical.

"I was tired of all the stress and wanted something insignificant for a change."

"So you decided to be a chef?"

"I was supposed to chop vegetables, a mindless task I could do in my sleep. Chopping vegetables turned into pressing garlic and peeling potatoes and making pesto and… restaurants are a lot more stressful than you would think."

"Of course, they are. How long did you last?"

"A little less than two weeks, but I learnt their pesto and alfredo sauces…"

"And mix the two together." I understood how he got his pesto so cheesy.

"My Gift should have been sharing it with the world," he teased.

"Definitely," I agreed. "What other jobs have you done?"

"Way too many to count. I migrate around the same general idea, but you can't stay too long when you look like this." He shrugged. I wanted to ask more, but didn't get the feeling he wanted to talk about it.

"I see nothing wrong with the way you look," I teased.

"Some people managed to look past my appearance and see my worth, but they were few and far between. Probably my fault though. I wasn't very trusting."

"A bit of a lone wolf?" I tied my hair into a messy knot at the top of my head. The oven, the stove, the pasta, and the summer air were all contributing to make the kitchen very hot.

"Not on purpose. One of my first jobs outside of the family was as a day laborer in a factory. All the other men got close, eating lunch together, drinking at night...making friends. I, on the other hand, spent my lunches getting ahead on work, and didn't need to see them in the evenings because if I wanted someone to drink with, I had Embry."

"Loyal with the one best friend." It was like me with Keisha, only that wasn't entirely by choice.

"It wasn't intentional. I just didn't feel a need to make friends, which seems to be something I need to work at to achieve."

"You got Terrence," I argued.

"That was all him."

"You've spent the past three centuries not getting close to anyone because you already had a best friend, even if you weren't talking to him anymore?" I verified.

"When you put it that way...some people managed to get in." He looked at me purposely before clearing his throat. "It was usually more subconscious on my part."

"I am really glad you're back to being friends then."

"When did you find out about him and Beth?" he asked.

"I saw it when we first got here." I didn't want him to think I'd been keeping it from him for years. "But I was pregnant with Jack when I fell out of the tree. Beth was," I corrected myself.

"That must be weird."

"It is," I agreed. "It's really weird, surreal, terrible, and incredibly awesome, all at the same time."

"Do you think there's a point to it?"

"There has to be, not that I can see it. None of the others had memories like this? Not even once?"

"The only ones with supernatural abilities were Beth and Annabelle. Beth never confided in me – about anything, and Annabelle was the original, so there wouldn't have been memories for her."

. . .

ONCE WE WERE DONE with supper, I made cookies. We had all the ingredients, except chocolate chips, so I used M&Ms.

"Not going to warn me about salmonella?" I asked when Gabriel came over and ate one of the balls of cookie dough I had on a cookie sheet while the oven preheated.

"I think that was a real threat when it started, but things don't go bad anymore, they last forever. If Gaston eats five dozen raw eggs for breakfast, what can it hurt if you add some milk, sugar, and flour?" he asked, discovering the much larger quantity of dough I left in the mixing bowl.

"Was that a Beauty and the Beast reference?" I was shocked. "I wouldn't peg you as the fairytale romance type."

"Are you kidding? I was the hopeless romantic who wanted nothing more than to settle down and raise a family."

"That was your dream?"

"Still is. I just stopped believing it would come true a couple hundred years ago." He shrugged as if he didn't care, but I could see otherwise.

"I thought you were waiting..." I was leaning with my back against the oven, but I don't think that was why the room felt like it was a hundred degrees. Gabriel hadn't stepped back since his last dough venture, so I was acutely aware of how close he was. How easy it would be to reach out and...I swallowed, sincerely hoping my thoughts weren't written all over my face.

"I've known a long time that she wasn't coming back. It's probably the first rule in your magic books."

"You can't bring back the dead," I agreed, more from movies than my books.

"I grew up and understood that the things I wanted back then, that I would want now, like getting married, having kids, raising a family, and being happy...they're not real. They're fairytales."

"You've got a pretty good heart from what you accidentally let show. And you're not horrible to look at. I mean, you might have to adopt, but it could still happen," I told him nervously, putting my hand on top of his.

"I'm broken, Lucy," he argued, but he didn't take his hand away. He looked into my eyes with that intensity only he could bring, where it felt like he could see down to my very soul. "You wouldn't want me," he cut through the subtext of our conversation, but didn't look away. Just raw and vulnerable in front of me.

"You don't have to be." I looked right back into his eyes, black ones that still managed to have depth and kindness in them. My heart was beating a mile a minute and he was so close...it was like time was frozen, with just the two of us in the kitchen, and nothing else mattered. I could hear my heart as he came closer, the electricity tangible. I held my breath, not on purpose, but because I knew that the tiniest disruption would end this spell.

"I'm sorry." He kissed the top of my head, then pulled away and walked off without another word.

CHAPTER TWENTY-ONE

Gabriel didn't come back, so I went upstairs and got ready for bed. I caught sight of my reflection in the mirror and wished I didn't look like her. But then I wouldn't look like me either.

I read a few more chapters of the book on magic, learning that emotions, like love, were the most powerful, and that love, hatred, and fear could deeply impact spells and potions. Which was great for me, because I happened to be feeling all of them.

I really wanted to track Clara and Deanna, or even Keisha, just to feel them and know they were okay, but this wasn't an emergency, and I wouldn't want people peeking into my life when I thought I was alone.

I stared at the ceiling, unable to sleep for the longest time, finally deciding to open my window to get a little fresh air. That helped, but it would be a long time until I got to sleep.

"You're killing it, Luce." Sam was sitting in the corner of the room, his face beaming with pride.

"How are you here?" I asked, looking around for Ingrid. She

hadn't haunted me yet, but I had often wondered why she wasn't constantly hounded by people asking her to bring back their loved ones, at least for a little while. It might drive her crazy in the long run, but she could have an imaginary Beth hang out with her all day, looking, feeling, and sounding like the real thing.

"I'm always here for you. Until the end of time," he brought up the promise he made me after his dad's funeral.

"I'm dreaming," I understood, wanting to run to him and take advantage of him being there, even in a dream, but my dreams tended to turn into nightmares when Sam was in them.

"He can't get us here," Sam said, reading my thoughts.

"He can. He does all the time," I argued.

"Not tonight," he assured me.

"How would you know?"

"Because I've got you. If anyone bad shows up, you can freeze them or blow them up...you've got this." He smiled.

"I appreciate your confidence."

"But you don't trust it."

"I want to."

"But you don't want to be responsible if someone gets hurt. You would rather freeze or fail at some other kind of self-defense."

"You're acting like I would rather die..."

"Wouldn't you?" he called me out.

"If I could go back and take your place..."

"I would never let you."

"I would do it. A million times," I said over him.

"I know you would, but I'm the big brother, so I couldn't let you."

"They were after me. They wouldn't have been anywhere near you if it wasn't for me."

"But I was always going to do whatever I could to protect you."

"You had a family. Deanna and Clara will never forgive me."

"And you're mad at me," he called me on it.

"I'm not..." I looked at him and knew he was right. "Of course, I'm mad at you. You left me here and... you died for me."

"I didn't just die for you," he tried to downplay it.

"You fought and died so they wouldn't get me. Now I have to go home and tell your wife and daughter that I'm the reason you're gone."

"And you can't give up," he brought up a big reason why I was mad at him. "I died protecting you, so if you die, it's like I died for nothing. You can't give up when things get hard or refuse to do spells that scare you, because I died so you could live, and now you have to live."

"I hate you," I said, my eyes full of tears.

"I love you too." He opened his arms so I could go in for a hug.

"Are you only okay with this because you're a figment of my imagination?"

"No, I'm pissed off as hell," he said, his red hair glistening in the moonlight, but I saw a hint of his mother's fierceness in his eyes.

"I'm sorry," I said, mostly for causing his demise, but also for asking and upsetting him.

"The difference is that I'm not mad at you. I don't blame you for any of it."

"Not a single thing?" I called him on his lie.

"Silly things that don't matter anymore, like you and Deanna watching that doctor show without me when you know I can't admit that I like it. For growing up so fast and making me feel old. For those times when Clara asked you to read her the bedtime story instead of me." He put his hand under my chin to make me look at him. "But I don't lose sight of who I'm really mad at. I died because if Donovan got what he wanted, he was going to kill Clara and Deanna, and everyone like them. He's the real bad guy. That's who I'm mad at for a lot of things."

"I miss you. So much." It didn't need to be said, but I needed to tell him.

"I miss you too," he agreed. "Do you think you can forgive me for leaving you alone and not letting you take the easy way out of this?"

I sighed and paused, considering it. "I don't really have a choice, do I?"

"Not really," he agreed.

"Then you're forgiven." I gave him a sad smile, knowing he wasn't the one who needed forgiveness.

"Then I can give you your birthday present."

"You really don't have to." I was pretty sure I couldn't take things with me from my dream. "Just seeing you...this is perfect," I said of the hug.

"The present's better." He brought me back over to the bed, where he proceeded to tuck me in, securing the corners like he hadn't done for me in years. "Are you ready?" he asked, sitting on the edge.

I wanted to say no, because I knew he would be leaving as soon as he was done, but I was worried he would have to leave anyway, so I nodded.

"I forgive you," he said, looking into my eyes so I could see he meant it. "For everything you have or will ever do. I forgive you." He kissed the top of my head, then stepped back, out of the light, and was gone.

I woke with a start and recognized the room, but it suddenly felt empty without Sam in it. Or I guess I felt empty. I saw on the alarm clock that it was two in the morning, so I tried to get back to sleep. Then I heard it.

"Lucy!" It was Sam's voice, as clear as when he was sitting in front of me in the dream, but it was coming from outside the window.

"Sam?" I got out of bed and went to see for myself. It was one thing to talk to him in a dream, but another to hear him when I was awake.

"Come on!" he called with a smile, standing beneath the window.

"You can't be here." My brain tried to process what was going on.

"But I am. Why don't you come see for yourself?" he suggested.

"Let me see your eyes," I called down. The guys would kill me if I fell into a trap.

"Green, like yours." He stood under a porch light and opened them wide, so I could see.

"I'm coming," I told him, putting on the riding boots from Charlie and a sweater, because that was all I had at the door.

"Took you long enough." Sam sounded and looked exactly like himself.

"This is one of those things where you wake up but you're still dreaming," I called him on it as if he were the one who tricked my brain into thinking I woke up.

"That does happen sometimes," he agreed.

"You should visit like this more often."

"How will you miss me if I never go away?"

"I don't want to miss you."

"Come on." He put out his hand. I followed him over to the stables, but then we walked around them towards the woods, and the swamps.

"It's faster by horse," I shared.

"I've never been a fan."

It was true. He was super allergic to any kind of animal. When Deanna found an abandoned puppy in the yard, we had to hide him from Clara and find a new home, because there was no way we'd ever be able to keep him.

"What adventure are you taking me on now?" I was glad I chose the boots. It would have been hard to keep up otherwise.

"It's a surprise." He smiled, daring me to figure it out.

"I'm not the biggest fan of surprises."

"You'll like this one." He picked up the pace and I started to see how much easier it was for Donner to hop over obstacles, like overturned trees, than it was for me to climb over them.

I wiped my muddy hands off on the back of my boxer shorts, where I usually dried them.

Sam was unusually quiet, helping me over fallen branches and pulling others back so I could get through, but the deeper we went, the more I started to think this maybe wasn't exactly what it seemed.

"Just a little bit farther," Sam said like he sensed my uncertainty.

"Can I get a hint?"

"It's something you've wanted a lot lately, but haven't told anyone," he said after considering it for a long time.

"But I didn't want it before?"

"Never even crossed your mind."

"I want it right now?" I questioned.

He paused, then looked at me like he wasn't so sure anymore. "You will," he told me.

We got to the clearing where Eric and I had stopped the first time he took me riding.

"I don't usually get eaten alive when I'm sleeping," I worried, slapping my thigh, yet again.

"Who says you're sleeping?" Sam asked, stepping into the muddy swamp.

"What are you doing?" I didn't like where this was going. At all.

"It's just past those trees there, in the bog." He pointed to a spot where I could see a light, but not much else.

"What is it?"

"Do you trust me?" he asked.

"Of course." Even as I said the words, I knew they were a lie. I trusted Sam more than anything in the world, but this wasn't my Sam.

"Then follow me." He put out his hand again, but this time I didn't take it.

"Why don't we go back to the house now. I can make us some tea and…"

"Don't you want us to be together?" he cut me off, looking so upset, before he pushed me into the swamp. I landed where it wasn't too deep yet, but he dragged me further into the water, his hands like claws around my arms.

CHAPTER TWENTY-TWO

"What are you doing?" I screamed at the man who looked like Sam, struggling to keep my head above water.

"It's okay Lucy, don't fight it, I've got you," he assured me.

"This isn't you," I argued, trying to get up.

"It's okay," Sam repeated, then came close to take me in for a hug.

He let himself sink to the bottom, which brought me down as well. I fought to stay up, but he was holding on to my arms, and my legs could only kick so much. I looked for something to grab onto, but we were in the middle of the swamp, which was surprisingly deep. I could swear I saw Gabriel coming for me in the distance, but I chalked it up as wishful thinking. Obviously, my mind would go *there*.

My head bobbed under for a moment, but I could clearly see Gabriel fifty feet away from me once I resurfaced. He had his hand out in front of him, like he was following someone I couldn't see.

"Lucy!" Gabriel spotted me in the swamp and called out, giving me hope that he wasn't a figment of my imagination.

"Gabriel!" I struggled to stay on top long enough to call out to him. I saw Embry step into the swamp, looking like he was in a daze, before I was pulled to the bottom again.

By the time I fought my way back to the surface, Gabriel was getting closer to me, but he kept having to pull something, or someone off his back to do it. I tried to swim to him, but my sweater was caught on something. When pulling didn't work and the material wouldn't rip, I took a deep breath and willingly went under to untangle myself. When I came up, it was dark, and I couldn't see Embry or Gabriel anywhere. I was wishing I'd brought a flashlight when the white light Sam pointed to earlier moved towards us. It lit up the swamp, but it also made me want to go back to the dark, when the ominous orb was farther away.

Fake Sam was gone, but there were still hundreds of what felt like winged mice trying to pull me down, so I used magic to get them off.

Fresh air never tasted so sweet, but I only let myself take two deep breaths before I called out to Embry and Gabriel. I still couldn't see them, but there were bubbles not far from me, so I swam over and pulled, which was enough for Gabriel to get his head above water.

"I can't." I could see him try to use his speed to get to me, but a gargoyle-like creature was digging its nails into his neck. I concentrated very hard on the creature and froze it, not trusting myself to do anything else when it was so close to Gabriel. "They're all over," he told me, struggling to get them off and stay above water.

No matter how many I blew up, more kept coming, trying to use my clothes and my hair to drag me down.

"You need to get out of the water," Gabriel shouted.

"I'm trying," I agreed. "Where's Embry?"

Gabriel ignored the creatures clawing at him and managed to swim close and take a few off me. He pulled me through the water, closer to the edge, which seemed so far away.

My heart nearly stopped when Embry burst out of the water a few feet away from Gabriel, but he went down as quickly as he came up. I could see more now that their numbers were growing, but it was more terrifying than reassuring.

I targeted individual creatures underwater, trying to help Embry, but I didn't trust my aim when he was squirming like that.

"Focus on you," Gabriel warned, knocking creatures off me while more dug into him.

"He's drowning, and you're barely staying up," I pointed out before one of them tugged on my leg. Embry and Gabriel's immortality wasn't an exact science, which meant there was a possibility that if the creatures killed them, they wouldn't come back.

Gabriel struggled harder to help me to a large branch while I blasted any that were close, until I had my arms around the thickest part.

"Don't move," he ordered before going under, I think intentionally, but it terrified me all the same.

I DID what I could with my powers, but there were so many of them, all over the guys, that by the time I could concentrate enough to target one, another replaced it.

"Embry!" I exclaimed when Gabriel grabbed hold of him, but they weren't out of danger yet. The white, orb-like structure above the bog seemed to be a hive with millions of them, waiting to come after us.

I tried to reach out, to give them my hand so they would have something to hold on to, but the creatures hadn't let up on me either. If I didn't have a good hold on the branch, I couldn't stay above water. I also couldn't get close enough to them without completely letting go.

Embry struggled to help Gabriel when he went under. When

Embry went down as well, I decided it wasn't worth me being safe if they drowned. I let go of the branch and tried to swim to them. If I could get close enough, I could blast the creatures around them.

I GOT SWARMED as soon as I was out of the branch's reach. It was like they knew I was the one who attacked them, so they attacked me with a vengeance to ensure it wouldn't happen again. I quickly changed course and got back to the branch, but this time I had an idea.

I climbed up a little higher on the tree-like structure, until my body was no longer in the swamp. The little creatures followed me, clawing into my skin, but at least I had a better view of what I was dealing with.

I took a deep breath and concentrated as hard as I could on levitating Gabriel and Embry, lifting them out of the water so they wouldn't drown. They came out coughing, which I took as a good sign, but I couldn't break my concentration.

"Just do it," Gabriel suggested when I tried to figure out a way to blast the creatures without hurting the guys. I was not going to let them die so I could save myself. Not again.

"I've got this," I argued with a confidence I didn't feel.

Gabriel looked at me like he wanted to argue and tell me to do as I was told, but he wasn't going to discourage me from saving them with magic.

The creatures were everywhere, attached to every inch of Embry and Gabriel, as well as my legs. I tried to focus on them, like I had with the sand, but there was no way I could get all of them at once.

I took another deep breath and held my moonstone necklace tight. I imagined all the little creatures as warm fireflies, giving light on summer nights, rather than leading mourning innocents to their deaths in the swamps. I pictured it with all my might until I slowly felt the claws leaving my body. I knew I was imagining the buzzing, but I heard it and felt warmth all around me, like the energy from a million fireflies.

I was terrified to look, because I didn't know if I would be able to turn Embry and Gabriel back if they were fireflies now. They definitely wouldn't regenerate if they weren't human.

WHEN I SLOWLY OPENED MY eyes, Embry and Gabriel were there, floating in the air, looking at all the fireflies with wonder.

"You did it." They looked as amazed as I felt.

"I thought you might be fireflies too," I admitted.

"I had more faith in you than that," Gabriel said as I floated them over to solid ground.

"No, you didn't," I argued. His solution had been for me to kill everyone and everything in the bog. I half-waddled, half-swam over to the shore with them.

"What were they?" Gabriel asked.

"Fee follet," I admitted. "They lure people into the swamps and drown them."

"The missing people Ingrid was worried about…" Embry ventured.

"We all fell for it," I defended them.

"You followed someone out here even after you knew this was a thing?" Gabriel was upset.

"I thought I was dreaming." They looked to me like that was nowhere near an acceptable excuse. "I know it was stupid, but Ingrid said they looked like floating lights. I wasn't expecting something that looked like Sam. They've clearly evolved because I wouldn't go anywhere with a floating light, but I would follow my real Sam to the end of the earth."

"You nearly did," Embry pointed out.

"I wasn't alone in that swamp, and it wasn't just because you were rescuing me," I threw it back at them.

"We were. At first," Embry said before they looked guiltily to each other.

"Point is, they shouldn't be bothering us anymore." Gabriel got us off the topic of how we all got duped.

"I don't know if it's permanent," I argued. "I don't know much when it comes to my powers."

"You knew enough to do that." Gabriel pointed back to the fireflies, clearly impressed, as we headed to the house.

"How did you come up with that?" Embry asked. "I don't think I've seen anyone actually turn something into something else. Other than Ingrid's illusions."

"I couldn't get rid of them, there were so many. I figured I wouldn't be able to individually destroy them all, but I could try something that would free you, but not kill you if it went wrong."

"I'm glad you didn't kill us." Embry smiled, wrapping his arm around me.

"Speaking of…" I confronted Embry once Gabriel was far enough ahead.

"I didn't nearly kill you," he took the defensive.

"No, you nearly killed you," I called him on it.

"I'm pretty sure we agreed that all of us got tricked."

"We did," I agreed. "But Gabriel and I realized something was wrong and fought back. You were down a really long time."

"I wasn't *trying* to die."

"But you're ready for it." He wasn't guilty or offended enough for it to not be the truth.

"Don't look so shocked." He didn't meet my eyes, but he was sure of himself. "I've lived centuries. Literally. I've fallen in love, I got married, I had children, I watched one of them get married and have a child of her own…I buried all of them. I won't be jumping into any swamps, or intentionally doing anything reckless, but when my time comes and I don't wake up…" he let the thought linger, and even though he made excellent points, I didn't like it.

"Do you think that's likely? I mean, for you to not come back, we either need to defeat the Big Bad, or I have to not be worth saving."

"I'm going with the first one," he said like the second wasn't an option.

"The fee came to you as Beth?" I asked him.

"Beth, Helen, and Jackson," he corrected.

"Everyone you love."

"Not everyone." He pulled me close.

"It would be really hard to not follow that," I let him know I understood.

"It was," he agreed. "But I wouldn't knowingly choose them over saving you."

"I'm pretty sure Lucy saved us this time," Gabriel rejoined our conversation.

"I raised you right," Embry teased.

"No, she would have stayed where I told her if you had."

"And we all would have drowned," Embry defended me.

"Which shows we all make mistakes sometimes." Gabriel gave me a look.

"What now?" I asked when we got to the house.

"Now? We sleep," Embry answered like I was crazy.

"What about the fee follet?"

"We'll have Ingrid come over tomorrow after we've all showered and had some sleep."

"Agreed." The smell and the cold were getting to me now that I wasn't dying.

We went upstairs, where Embry walked straight to the master bathroom without even saying goodnight.

"You can go first," Gabriel said awkwardly when we both headed for the common bathroom.

"Thank you." I went in while he headed downstairs, but I called him back, "Gabriel."

"Yes?" He lingered on the top step.

"Thank you for breaking out of it. I know how hard that must have been."

"She wasn't real. You are," he said simply.

"Goodnight."

"Goodnight."

CHAPTER TWENTY-THREE

Ingrid came over the following evening to see if the fee follet truly left us. Just to be sure, she came back every night that week, each time with a different group of paranormal beings. Mostly witches and warlocks, but one called herself a seer, one a druid, and another a leprechaun. Gabriel snickered under his breath for that one, but given the company we were keeping, it didn't seem that far-fetched. On the last day, instead of heading out to the swamps, Ingrid handed us a tiny envelope, smiled, and left.

"That was odd," Gabriel stated, waiting for me to open the envelope.

"There's a party in the quarter tonight to celebrate the end of the disappearances. She wants us to go, even if we can't be the guests of honor."

"Not a good idea," Gabriel argued.

"It's in the alley in front of her shop, which will be protected by every means possible to meet our stringent requirements," Embry continued reading from where I left off.

"Who else is going?"

"Please find enclosed the list of attendees." I handed him a second sheet from the envelope.

"I wish we had more time to make sure it would be safe…" Gabriel struggled with the decision.

"I'm pretty sure that's why she didn't give you any," I pointed out, completely understanding her smile and quick exit now.

"I don't have a choice in the matter, do I?"

"Of course you do. As long as you don't care whether or not we do what you choose," Embry teased.

"We're not staying long, and you're not leaving my sight," Gabriel warned.

"Of course," I agreed.

WE LEFT the villa at five so we could be at Ingrid's shop by six. It really wasn't that far distance-wise, but they liked to take precautions. The dress I brought was coming in handy in NOLA. I paired it with Ingrid's shawl in case it got chilly. The last time I got dressed up pretty to go somewhere was prom. I was no longer under any illusions about magic, or life working out for me, but I was excited at the prospect of spending a night out, where we could pretend my life wasn't extremely complicated and dangerous.

As SOON AS I walked into the alley, I got that horrible, yet familiar feeling of someone trying to get into my brain. I pushed him out immediately and heard Mr. Fraser's "Ow!" before Ingrid came over.

"I'm so glad you came." She took me in for a hug. "Come, there's food and drinks and people to meet…" She brought me through the party, where we were the last to arrive.

"This is my niece, Beth." Ingrid winked to me as she lied,

introducing me to a man who lost his father to the fee follet weeks before.

"You're very good at that," I pointed out once we were away from the crowd a bit.

"Talking to people?" she asked.

"Lying to them." Her face went dark, so I attempted to get my foot out of my mouth. "No, I mean it as a compliment. You didn't miss a beat when he asked who I was. You said it so seamlessly that I nearly believed you."

"You need to mix a little truth with the lies and commit," she advised. "Always remember what you tell people, because they do. Not all of them, but the day you mess up, they'll remember, and then it's over."

"Is everyone who's here…"

"Gifted? Of supernatural inclinations?" she finished for me. "No, some are friends of mine, others are people who've lost someone to the fee follet…It's not a magic party, it's a community party. It's very important to have friends from all walks of life."

"I'll remember that."

"Beth would be proud," she said out of nowhere. "I'm amazed at how well you've adapted to your powers. From fearing them to controlling them and experimenting…that's no easy feat."

"I wasn't experimenting," I argued.

"You just needed to save them." She gave me a knowing smile.

"Thank you for being here and helping me through it."

"Of course. It's not every day you get to practically go back in time and fix a mistake."

"What mistake?" I asked.

"I was so jealous of Beth when she was figuring it out that I was useless."

"I'm sure you made up for it."

"I think so. She was the best friend I ever had."

"What about Mr. Fraser?" I asked.

"He was a very different kind of friend."

"Who ran his course?"

"Are you implying he got old?" she played offended.

"Potion or no potion…"

"I was head over heels in love with that man, and he offered me all of it. His heart, a house, kids…but I knew what I was, what I could never be to him…"

"You turned him down?"

"I let him marry a woman instead of an eight-year-old girl." She still sounded upset by it.

"That's it?"

"He married Mrs. Fraser. Had children. Built a wonderful life…But he never stopped loving me."

"Are you together now?"

"Of course not. We keep each other company and pretend there's nothing there." Her words painted a sad and lonely existence of never getting what you want, but she said it in a no-nonsense manner.

"That sounds terrible."

"Love is strange, my dear. And it makes you do ridiculous things."

"Do you regret it?"

"I regret not having a happy ending." She sighed. "But I don't regret letting him have one. I would rather see him happy than sad, even if he isn't with me." She looked out onto the street, where there was a parade going on. "They have parades for everything here." She sighed after the bride came into view, but I heard a yearning for her own marriage procession before the party slipped away…

I WAS ANNABELLE, *so nervous, my heart beating out of my chest, possibly because of how small my gown was. I looked down and saw it was a wedding dress that bound me so tight.*

"It is quite an elaborate affair," Annabelle teased, as the hands fumbling with the back of my dress stopped.

"I'll figure out the corset," Henry said with determination. "I was transfixed by this." He ran his fingers over the back of my neck, sending shivers down my spine.

"It's a birthmark. I'm told it is a perfect half-moon," she said, trying to look back, to read his expression. All I saw was the top of his head, the perfectly coiffed hair suffering from the sweat and exertion of unlacing the dress.

"A crescent moon," Henry agreed, kissing the mark before going back to the dress.

While he unlaced her, occasionally planting a kiss as he worked his way down my back, Annabelle's hands twisted the wedding band around her finger. I could feel her excitement at starting a life with Henry, and her gratitude that he loved her in spite of her magic and other flaws. But there was a feeling in the pit of her stomach that was telling me this was a terrible mistake. I couldn't tell if it was her heart or mine that beat faster at the thought of Gabriel, but Annabelle struggled to push all other thoughts from her mind as the dress finally fell free, and she turned to face her groom...

"Are you okay?" Ingrid asked, her hand on my shoulder when I woke up.

"Did I pass out?" I asked.

"No, mostly stood there playing with your hands," she shared as I looked around to make sure people weren't staring. "You had a memory?"

"The wedding dress triggered something," I agreed, grateful I didn't have to explain it to her.

"It was a beautiful wedding." She gave me a smile, assuming I saw Beth with Embry, before Mr. Fraser came over. "I'm sorry about earlier. I've been scanning everyone to make sure you would be safe. I didn't know it was you."

"It's okay," I assured him, his earlier intrusion the last thing on my mind. "I'll go check out the food." I made my exit so they could keep each other company.

I WENT over to the food table, sorting through my thoughts to figure out what the memory was for, or if it was a fluke brought on by the dress. I decided Henry noticing the birthmark was worth a mention to the guys, before someone came up behind me and said, "Charlie brought the crawfish, so it's to die for, but the scallops have sand in them."

"I wasn't expecting to see you here." I turned to face Eric and took him in for a hug.

"Charlie and Ingrid go way back," he shared. "And he loves parties."

"I was referring to you being in school."

"Oh, that?" He shrugged it off.

"I was under the impression you only spent the summers in New Orleans."

"Usually," he agreed, getting me to blush again.

"Did you already eat?" I brought the attention back to the food.

"I did. But the crawfish..." He brought his fingers to his lips and kissed the air.

"Is to die for," I repeated his words back to him.

"You get it." He smiled.

"Is this your first of Ingrid's parties, or can you tell a newcomer what to expect?" I looked around, trying to see if anything other than eating, drinking, and talking was going on. Gabriel was laughing with Charlie and Embry, the three of them looking like they didn't have a care in the world, until Embry used two fingers to point to his eyes, then back to me. I rolled my eyes at him before coming back to Eric.

"I've been to a few," he told me. "One was in the streets and absolutely crazy, and the other was above her shop, with maybe five people, and twenty courses of fancy dishes with food."

"So no idea what to expect tonight," I concluded.

He sighed before looking at me and shaking his head slowly. "Not with the party."

"But with other things?"

"I maybe have an idea." He sounded more resigned than excited.

"Of something bad?"

"For me, yes. For you...I'm not sure yet." He tried to read me.

"Is it something with Charlie?" I looked over to the three men again, but they all seemed to be having the time of their lives.

"I think you're awesome Lucy. You're probably the fiercest, most badass woman I have ever encountered, and I like you. As friends, sure, but also as a lot more than friends. If I didn't think Embry and Gabriel would kill me for it, I would want to kiss you right now."

I could feel myself flush and got nervous. Terribly nervous. At first because I thought he was going to kiss me and I wouldn't be good at it, but then because I didn't think I wanted him to. That's when I looked at him and realized he had no intention of kissing me tonight.

"I would want to, except that I have no interest in kissing a girl who doesn't want to kiss me."

"I think you're amazing Eric. You're nice and funny and helpful..."

"But I don't make you swoon," he understood.

"You do..." I remembered how much I blushed when he took me riding for the first time.

"Not like he does." It was a weird role-reversal where I felt like he was the one letting me down easy. "And it's okay… I see the way you look at him, mostly when you know he isn't watching, how jealous he gets about us hanging out, that fight he had with Embry…"

"What fight?" I was about to argue with his previous comments, to defend myself, but the guys were finally friends. I didn't want to have to wait another three hundred years for them to make up again.

"The big fight that had them refusing to talk to each other for at least a week."

"That was about Annabelle. Gabriel thought Embry was trying to insert himself based on loving Annabelle, but it was because he loved Beth," I explained, but Eric looked at me like I look at Clara sometimes when she doesn't understand things that are so obvious to everyone else.

"Maybe Gabriel was upset about that, but the storming off was because of you. Embry saw it too, so he told him not to hurt you like he hurt Rosie, and Gabriel said he didn't understand, that it wasn't like that."

"You remembered all that?" I tried to process what it meant.

"It didn't make sense until you told me about the ones that came before you."

"None of it makes sense," I argued, getting a look from Eric to stop arguing on this. "I'm sorry," I said, for not liking him like that, for liking Gabriel, who I'm pretty sure will break my heart…

"Don't be. Proximity doesn't equal love. It doesn't even guarantee friendship."

"But we are friends, right?" I asked, worried it might be cruel, but I couldn't deal with the alternative.

"If you want to be."

"I do."

"Then we're friends."

"Is that mean?"

"If you had let me kiss you and I had to wait for you to come clean about your feelings, that would have been cruel," he said, but he was smiling.

"You're really awesome. You know that?"

"I do," he assured me. He took one of the crawfish from my plate and ate it with a huge smile that told me we were going to be okay.

CHAPTER TWENTY-FOUR

We stayed at the party another hour or so, which included some dancing and a heartfelt rendition of 'My Way' from Charlie, that garnered a standing ovation. He and Ingrid insisted the party couldn't possibly go on without us, but we weren't even done saying goodbye before they got right back to partying.

Eric smiled at me from across the tables before we walked to the car.

"What was that about?" Embry asked me while Gabriel drove.

"What?" I asked like I had no idea, but I knew exactly what he was referring to.

"Did something happen between you and Eric?" Embry raised an eyebrow.

"He's back at school now." I shrugged, pretty sure I was blushing, but I didn't want to talk about it with Gabriel in the car.

"What does that mean for the two of you?" he pressed.

"That we're friends. And we'll see each other less often. Possibly never again, or every summer for the rest of our lives."

Embry rolled his eyes. "Is that the plan if they never find us? To live in the villa forever? Because so far whatever Beth did seems to be working, or they're planning something big and scary and luring me into a false sense of security, which is not cool," I voiced some of my fears.

"I'll make sure to tell them next time I see them," Gabriel assured me.

"I am partly serious."

"We want to keep you safe for as long as possible, so we can train you and hone your skills."

"To give me a chance at surviving the next encounter."

"And live happily ever after." Embry smiled back at me before a man ran across the street, right in front of our car like he didn't even see it.

Gabriel slammed on the brakes, propelling me forward. I would have gone through the front window if I wasn't wearing my seatbelt. Thankfully, I don't think the impact was strong enough to kill anyone.

"Are you okay?" Embry poked his head out to address the man once he made sure I was unharmed, but Gabriel was fuming.

"I'm so sorry, I wasn't thinking. I just saw—"

"A car coming, and thought you would run in front of it? I could have killed you, we all could have died here," Gabriel pointed out.

"I know, of course..." the man was apologetic and frazzled until he spotted me in the car. For a moment I thought it hit him how many lives he put in danger, but he looked right into my eyes, and I could see something click for him.

"Gabriel..." I tried to tell him to leave, that I had a bad feeling about this, but I could see the black in the man's eyes, and knew it was too late.

Without taking his eyes off me, the man put his hands on the hood of our car. I thought it was a means of preventing us from running him over on purpose, but the black hood turned red, spreading from his hand to cover the rest of it in melting metal. It wasn't long until the engine was smoking, outside at first, but then through the vents, as the car overheated.

By the time we got out of the car, part of the hood was melting. The man had one hand up, palm facing us in a way that suggested he might be able to blast the heat out of it and incinerate us.

"Lucy Owens. Fancy running into you here," he said cockily while the guys glared at him, and I stood frozen in fear. "You must be her faithful lapdogs, Embry and Gabriel?"

I kept thinking how the guys were weaponless. It didn't even occur to me that the man was outnumbered by us, or that I had magical powers. Not until Embry, who was standing with Gabriel between me and the man, reached his hand back to take mine and said, "You've got this."

My magic hadn't occurred to me because this was a person, not a creature or a monster without a face. The man kept talking about how excited Donovan would be, while I took a deep breath and prepared to use my powers against him. Freezing him would be hard to explain if anyone came by, but it wasn't like I was going to blow him up either.

"Daddy!" I jumped, as did the man, when a toddler ran out from a driveway and rushed into his arms.

"Hey buddy. I thought I told you to wait for me at the corner, before crossing the street." He kept his eyes on me while talking to the boy, daring me to proceed with my attack.

"Lucy…" Gabriel said through clenched teeth.

"I can't."

"He's bigger than the rice," Embry pointed out.

"I can't do it in front of his son," I argued. Even if I could control it.

"He doesn't look like he cares." Gabriel nodded to the man,

who had his hand out, ready to fire at us even with his son in his arms.

"I can't…" I was still shaking my head when the man shot a blast of magma in our direction. I put my shield up before it reached us, but it was a very close call.

"We need to get her to the villa. Preferably the panic room," Embry voiced.

"We can't leave and let him make contact," Gabriel argued.

"What about the kid?" They both looked at me before exchanging a look that made me feel like a naïve child.

"I don't want to lie to you," Gabriel said delicately.

"Then don't."

"Whatever it takes, Lucy." He sighed, not meeting my eyes.

"Can you keep this up while we move?" Embry asked me.

"I'm not leaving," I argued. No children were dying on my behalf.

"Lucy…" Embry used his paternal tone on me.

"How long would it take you to get to him" I asked Gabriel.

"What are you doing?" I took the pen Eric gave me from my purse.

"If the man gets knocked out, will you be able to get to the boy before he hits the ground?" I rephrased my question.

"Of course," Gabriel looked at the tiny needle in my hand with concern.

I wasn't sure how much I trusted my aim at this distance, so instead of shooting it as intended, I used one hand to keep up my force shield, and levitated the needle so it nearly skimmed the ground, unnoticed, until it was less than an inch from the man's foot.

"Ready?" I asked Gabriel, who nodded. "Now," I said, stabbing the man with the toxin-filled needle. He looked down with a slight jerk of his leg, like he'd been stung by a bee, before he fell. Gabriel was barely a blur before the man was on the ground and Gabriel was standing there with the crying boy in his arms.

. . .

WITHOUT A WORD, Embry went over and took the child, who stopped crying immediately, resting his head on Embry's shoulder like he'd known him forever. Gabriel knelt to the ground and went through the man's pockets, finding a driver's license.

"He lives two streets that way." He pointed off in the distance.

"What are we going to do with him?" I asked, hoping there was a mother or someone at the house who could take care of the kid. Maybe we could keep injecting the man with the toxin until we got away from here. I was about to interrupt their exchange of looks with my suggestion, but Gabriel's eyes grew wide as he pulled something out of another pocket.

"Did he reach anyone?" Embry asked, recognizing it as a pager before I did.

"Can you even tell?" I got a head shake from Gabriel in return.

"We need to get out of here as soon as possible," Embry decided.

"If he knows we're here he'll go straight to your place," Gabriel warned.

"I didn't bring my bag," I admitted. I got too comfortable here and prepared for tonight like I was any other girl going to a party. "Do you have a map?" I did the mental math to see how long it would take someone to get here from California. They both shook their heads.

"You can't go there," Embry argued, accurately reading my determination.

"We need to know if he's on to us, right?"

"What is she doing?" Gabriel asked before I clutched the moonstone necklace and closed my eyes, picturing Donovan's face. I embraced the fear and the chill in my spine, hoping I would see him thousands of miles away, unaware that anything happened.

"*Richard's new, but I trust him.*" *I zeroed in on Donovan, who seemed to be in a garden.*

"*New Orleans is risky on their part, but not entirely unexpected,*" *a voice answered from behind a vine. It was oddly familiar.*

"*Does that mean you'll be joining me?*" *Donovan asked, his head slightly bowed in deference to who must be his master.*

"*You're going yourself?*" *There were very few people I knew with British accents. Most of them were movie stars, but I could feel my heart tighten in my chest as I placed this one.*

"*I want to be the one to bring her to you, my lord.*"

"*There's no need. She'll find us eventually.*" *He stepped out from behind the leaves and my heart stopped. The expression was different, but the face was otherwise unchanged from the last time I saw it, smiling at me in my wedding dress.*

"*We might not have time for her to figure it out,*" *Donovan argued with as much respect as the words would allow.* "*I'll take the jet and keep you informed.*"

"*Unharmed,*" *Henry warned, looking straight at me. It was impossible, but...he saw me.*

"Are you okay?"

"Are they coming?"

Gabriel and Embry looked at me with concern, but I couldn't reassure them. I couldn't breathe. It felt like my heart was breaking.

"Did he do something to you?" Embry asked.

"Donovan is taking a jet from Salem." I felt the street going blurry and fought it long enough to tell them we were momentarily safe, before I slipped away...

.   .   .

"WHAT IS THIS?" Annabelle asked Henry, holding very old pages in her hand. I wanted to warn her when she said it with curiosity rather than suspicion, but then I saw the look on his face. The smile he looked up at her with had gone dark, the sparkle disappearing from his eyes as his jaw set.

"You weren't supposed to find that," he said, coming closer. With every step he took in our direction, I got more afraid, until he got close enough to take the paper from her. She flinched, and though she didn't know what she was afraid of, I did. Henry reacted to the flinch as if she slapped him.

"A few words on a piece of paper and already you're afraid of me?" he asked, hurt.

"A few words combined with a lot of secrets, long absences, and I question how well I know you," she argued, taking a step back. "The heart of the Bearer of the Crescent Moon?" she pressed.

"An ingredient in the ritual I was put on this world to complete," he admitted.

"A ritual for what?" Annabelle was disgusted more than afraid, but I was terrified.

"To become more powerful than anyone else on earth," Henry said with a hint of hope, like this might entice her.

"Like a king?" she asked, but she knew that wasn't it. With the magic Henry was capable of, he was already more powerful than the men who held powerful positions in this country and every other.

"More powerful than all the kings and rulers and everyone else put together," he said with a gleam in his eye, which had never looked so cold before.

"All it takes is my heart?" She remembered the first time he mentioned her birthmark, after the wedding. Annabelle wondered the same thing I did; had he perhaps glimpsed it on that first day, before he decided to intervene on her behalf?

"Don't look at me like that Annie, this ritual is why I am here on earth," he pleaded, so unlike what I expected from Donovan's master.

"You've always had these grand ideas, always needed more instead of being happy with what you have."

"I don't want more, I need it. I need it, or I die trying. That's the way it has to be."

"Says who?" she asked. We were nearly in the doorway now.

"Death shall not claim me while I am on the chosen path," he admitted.

"What?" It sounded like he was repeating a passage from a book rather than giving an answer.

"There are people put on this world to accomplish certain tasks. I was put here to complete the ritual, and as long as I am still working on it, until I have achieved it, I cannot die. You can pierce my heart as many times as you like and tomorrow, I will wake up as if nothing happened. I've done it at least a dozen times before."

"You've died?" She tried to process this new information, that went far beyond the little bits of magic he did with her. I was shocked it wasn't hundreds of times, based on how dark his eyes had become.

"You'd be surprised how many people choose to stand in the way of others accomplishing their dreams, rather than helping them along the way. Not to mention those who have the same dream and are jealous because I am the only one to find a way."

"A way to do what?" I noted the fear in her voice as she failed to recognize the man she married.

"To rule the world. Once the ritual is complete, nothing will be able to stop me."

"And my death is a price you are willing to pay?" I could feel her heart breaking as if it were my own.

"Your death would most likely be temporary, my love. I would be so powerful that the laws of heaven and hell, death and resurrection, would mean nothing to me. I could bring you back."

"Your eyes," Annabelle realized. "I should have known as soon as I saw your eyes."

"They sometimes get a little darker when I die, but it is hardly anything to..."

"A little darker? It was no accident, Henry, not a small price to pay for coming back to life. The darkness is spreading, and evil is devouring your soul. That is what is happening to your eyes. You're becoming a monster!" She was in the middle of the last word when his hand shot up and collided with her cheek. I felt the sting before she brought her hand up, more as a reflex than from the pain. All Annabelle felt was numb.

"Watch your tongue," Henry warned, the hatred in his voice doing nothing but prove her right.

"Or maybe you already were a monster, and I was too blind to see it."

"I am offering you the world on a silver platter. You dare question me when you should be showing gratitude and promising me your everlasting devotion? I will be a god." He believed it, but he also knew she wouldn't feel the same; it was evident on his face.

"You'll be a demon. A vile creature that sacrifices whatever it takes to stay on top, a sad excuse for a human being, let alone a god." She turned and headed for a room to our left. I could hear the baby crying.

"Where are you going?" Henry yelled after us.

"I am taking my daughter and getting as far away from you as I possibly can. You dare come after us, or I see you anywhere near her..." She called out of the room, stuffing piles of cloth into a bag while trying to soothe the tiny infant in the crib.

"You can't leave me. You were nothing when I found you. About to be raped by common thieves. You leave now, and you can never come back," Henry threatened. "You are shocked, this wasn't how I planned to tell you, but if you walk out that door, you are no longer my wife, you are just the Bearer of the Crescent Moon..."

I could feel a chill down my back, knowing what those words meant, but Annabelle pushed the fear aside and lifted Margaret from the crib. "I assure you; I want nothing more than to be rid of you," she told him once we were out of the nursery, heading for the door without even looking at him.

"You misunderstand me, Annabelle. I will let you walk out the *door, because that part of it is a test, but I won't let you leave." We froze. I could feel my heart pounding in my ears, but I could have sworn it stopped altogether.*

"You come anywhere near my daughter, and I will kill you." We turned to face him, Annabelle standing her ground now that her daughter was involved.

"She is my daughter as well," Henry fumed. "I have just told you that you can stab me or do what you want but I will not stay dead. I will come and find you."

"You might not be able to die, but I can," Annabelle threatened, taking out her dagger.

"I don't need you to be alive to rip your heart out," Henry warned.

"But I'm guessing it puts a damper on your plans if the heart in question has a dagger in it." I envied her bravery more than anything as I felt the tip of the cold blade on my chest. There wasn't a doubt in my mind that she would go through with it.

"You wouldn't kill yourself," he argued.

"Try me." She kept his stare. "Take one step closer and I will drive this through my heart."

"I will find you. I will hunt you down and then I will cut your heart out of your chest while you still breathe," he threatened, shocking her with his hatred.

"Haven't you already done that?" Annabelle asked before walking out of the house.

She kept the point of her dagger against her breast, right above her heart. Once we were a few houses away, she brought the dagger to her side, but she kept it out until we were safely at a church. I was amazed at how calm and confident she was when she told the priest she needed a carriage to get to Boston, even more so when he lent her his personal one. Once we could no longer see the church in the distance, Annabelle broke down and let the emotions out.

"Until the next town," she said under her breath. That was how long she gave herself to dwell on it before she was going to gather herself, make a plan, and be strong, like her daughter needed...

CHAPTER TWENTY-FIVE

I woke up with tears pouring down my face and no idea where I was. The crash occurred only a few streets from the villa, but I was still surprised I was out long enough for them to bring me back to what I assumed was Embry's. The closet of the master bedroom by the looks of it.

I went to the door and pounded on it, but nothing I did moved it in the slightest. I took the moonstone necklace in my hand and tried to see Embry, or Gabriel, but it was like something was blocking me. I could make things float inside the room, but the metal doors did more than keep the outside world from getting in.

I tried not to panic, telling myself the guys wouldn't just leave me in here. I had been so curious about Embry's 'treasures', but at the moment I didn't really care. If I let my mind wander it went straight to Henry, who seemed so sweet, but was actually the Big Bad who has been hunting my family for centuries. I wanted to believe that the guys didn't tell me because they didn't know, but I wasn't that naïve.

I tried to find a secret passage, or an alarm I could pull to let them know I was awake. I pulled every single book on the shelves, but I guess that only works in movies. If Donovan wasn't on his way to us, I could have spent hours reading each of the antique books, but I needed to find a way out.

There was a sheet covering what looked like frames in the corner, but I lifted it, to be sure. The first one was a life-size portrait of Annabelle, with Embry's initials in the corner. He used to bring me paintings when he would visit, or an easel and canvas he could fill while I read by the creek. He tried to get me into it as well, but it wasn't long until we discovered that painting was not something I excelled at. I could make really advanced kindergarten-level paintings that never went outside the lines, but that was about it. Embry, on the other hand, made Annabelle completely lifelike, in every aspect. I would guess that he painted it from memory, or before Annabelle left for Salem, because there was no way she could keep such a carefree smile after finding out she was married to a monster.

I could sort of see what Grams meant about the smiles letting you tell my ancestors apart. The next frame held Rosalind, but I could tell it was her even before I recognized her dress. Cassie was next, looking absolutely elegant, but also fierce. The last painting was of Beth, looking at the world with as much love and happiness as on her fifth anniversary with Embry. I wonder if she knew who we're all descended from.

There was nothing else there besides a few landscapes. When I grabbed the sheet to throw it back onto the frames, I knocked over some papers, revealing a red panic button. Since I was already in the panic room, I would assume it was designed to alert the authorities. Knowing Embry and the type of dangers he might need the room for, I didn't think his worked the same.

I PRESSED THE BUTTON, expecting an alarm to go off, but nothing happened. I pressed again and was beginning to think it wasn't connected to anything when the metal door opened to reveal Gabriel.

"Good, you're awake." He tried to come close, but I took a step back.

"I've packed your things and we're ready to go." Embry started talking as soon as he got close, before finally looking at me.

"We're not leaving," I argued.

"You told us Donovan was on his way. That gives us six hours, tops," Gabriel reminded me.

"He's on his way here, where he will find Charlie and Eric, defenseless. We can't keep running away and letting other people deal with the consequences." My hatred wasn't exactly directed at them, but I wasn't going to let Charlie and Eric join the ranks of Terrence, Caleb, and Sam so I could get away.

"I understand that you're upset, but sacrificing yourself doesn't protect anyone," Embry said gently.

"It actually protects everyone, but I wasn't planning on dying. Considering Donovan is coming alone, I was under the impression we were going to stop running. To stay here and fight. Or was that a lie too?"

"What did you see?" There was a hint of fear in their voices. I wondered if they knew exactly what I found out or were trying to figure out which of their many lies I was referring to.

"Luce…" Gabriel pressed.

"Don't Luce me," I warned.

"What happened?" He didn't back down.

"The Big Bad."

"He's here?" Embry was horrified.

"Part of him." There was venom in my words, and in my blood, as the anger coursed through me. The fear didn't leave their faces until they understood what I meant, and even then, they didn't own up to it.

"We don't…"

"You know exactly what I'm referring to. You've known all along," I reproached. "I've been seeing her memories. Annabelle's. After she left you guys, she moved to Salem on her own, where she eventually met this guy, Henry, who saved her from a group of thugs on the side of the road. He was the one who showed her that she had magic. He taught her how to use it, and eventually, he married her." By now there was no denying it.

"Luce..." Embry tried, but he couldn't meet my eyes.

"Did it slip your mind that the evil man we're running from, who hunts my family and caused Sam's death was my great-great-many-times-great-grandfather?"

Embry opened his mouth and tried a bunch of excuses before deciding to reason with me. "How would that help you?" he asked.

"You didn't think I deserved to know?" I asked instead. "What kind of person...I never met my dad, so I don't know if this is standard father-daughter behavior, but there has to be something entirely messed up about us if we come from that. He's a psychopath, and that stuff is genetic." I was angry at everyone who kept it from me, at Annabelle for not seeing through him, at him for being evil... I felt dirty.

"There is nothing wrong with you Lucy. Henry is a horrible man. Annabelle realized that and brought her daughter away from him to keep her safe. He is Margaret's father, yes, but I raised that little girl, and there was nothing evil or psychotic about her, just like there is none of that in you," Embry said with an intensity I usually associated with Gabriel.

"How could you not tell me? When I started having the dreams, you had to know I would eventually find out." I felt betrayed and heartbroken. I wanted to get angry, to have any other emotion overwhelm the pain that kept making me cry.

"It's not like he had any paternal instincts towards you.

Bringing up the connection would not have made him treat you any better. It would just make it harder for you to do what you have to in order to get away from him."

"Because I'm weak?"

"Because you have a heart. You care about people. We couldn't risk you coming face to face with Henry and letting him kill you because you couldn't harm a twisted kind of father figure," Embry corrected.

"Is that why Annabelle let herself die? Because she couldn't fight him, and she couldn't let him have her?"

"Annabelle would have killed him if she had the chance." Gabriel sounded so sure of himself, but I don't think he ever actually saw them together.

"Annabelle didn't fight the conviction, and she let them burn her at the stake because she knew it was all done on Henry's orders. If she fought it, or waited for a trial, it would give him enough time to come find her and Margaret. She admitted her guilt and let the flames take her so he wouldn't get what he needed. I think she thought it ended with her." Embry looked to Gabriel for confirmation on the last part, and he nodded with conviction.

"Not even close." I shook my head, biting my bottom lip.

"Let's get in the car and talk about this," Embry suggested.

"There's nothing to talk about. You've been lying to me my entire life and it never ends. I don't need to hear your lies because I don't believe them. I don't trust either of you anymore." They'd both stepped towards me, but I crossed my arms and took another step back.

"Lucy, everything we have ever done was to keep you safe," Embry pleaded.

"That's what you tell yourself." I shook my head. "But you were just lying and hurting me." I couldn't even look at them. "I need to clear my head, and then we are going to face Donovan and stop acting like cowards." I tried to channel Annabelle's confidence as I walked past them to exit the panic room, but my insides felt seconds away from a meltdown.

CHAPTER TWENTY-SIX

I wandered around the property for a bit before finding myself in the stables. I got some treats from the bucket and was feeding Rudolph when I heard someone come up behind me. I knew it wasn't Donovan yet, so I debated whether I should yell at Embry and Gabriel to go away or hear them out. When I turned around, it was Charlie.

"I'm sorry, I didn't mean to scare you," he said when I jumped. "You're not planning on riding out in the middle of the night, are you?"

"Of course not. I was wandering around and found myself here." I tried to give him a convincing smile. "Trouble sleeping?"

"I came to turn off the lights. I was going to leave when I saw you, but you looked like you could use some company. I've been told I am excellent at listening, if ever you want to talk."

"Not really," I admitted, but I didn't want to be alone either. "You could tell me more stories, if you don't mind?"

"Are we trying to avoid talking about something else?" he asked.

"Yes." I chose honesty.

"I know all about these. I'm supposed to find a way to tell a story that perfectly reflects what is going on with your life now, so by the time the story is over, you know what you need to do."

"That would be quite the skill." I gave him a small smile. "I don't think there's much I can do about the fact that the people I trusted the most lied to me." I didn't want to talk about it, but the pain and anger were so close to the surface. It wasn't even that I was mad...I felt betrayed and alone, like I didn't know anything anymore.

"One lie doesn't erase a lifetime—"

"Of lies," I cut off Charlie's words of wisdom. "They would come and visit me and make me feel special. I thought of Embry as family, but they've been lying to me since the day I met them. They're here to protect me, but if it comes down to it, they would rather stop him than save me, and I don't blame them, considering what's inside of me." The thought had been gnawing at me since Donovan mentioned it in the motel parking lot, but I had refused to believe it until now.

"I can't vouch for Gabriel, but Embry would give anything to see you safe and happy. He loves you more than anything else in this world."

"Love and duty are not the same thing," I said quietly.

"He wouldn't spend fifteen years talking my ear off about how wonderful you are if you were just an obligation," he argued. "Every spelling bee and class award, when you climbed to the top of the oak tree, when you made the best chocolate chip cookies he's ever tried...He has spent the last fifteen years telling me how proud he is of you, and showing me how much he loves you."

"Maybe both are true," I suggested.

"Maybe," he agreed.

I looked at him, trying so hard to help me without knowing what was going on. I took a deep breath and admitted, "The Big

Bad who is hunting us and has been trying to kill my ancestors for generations was actually married to Annabelle. The first one," I added in case he didn't know. "We all come from him."

He nodded, digesting the information, before he said, "Maybe they kept it from you because they love you and didn't want to hurt you, or risk you getting hurt?"

I was surprised by his reaction. "It's still lying to me," I pointed out. "About everything."

"About a tiny detail that only feels like everything because you just found out about it. I don't think your ancestry changes anything."

"It's the entire reason we're here. People are literally dying because of it," I pointed out.

"Because you're a strong and fierce Owens woman. Not because one asshole slipped his way into the family tree." I was surprised by the bluntness of his language. "I don't know if you're worried this means you're a bad apple, or have something dark and dangerous inside you, but I knew your Grams her whole life, and there wasn't an ounce of evil inside her, regardless of who her great-great-grandfather was."

"You don't think that giving someone superpowers to stay alive until they kill me means something?"

"You don't know what his purpose is," he reminded me, implying he knew way more about everything than I ever gave him credit for.

"I know what he thinks it is."

"Villains often get confused about what they're supposed to do," Charlie said with a smile and a wink that got me smiling too. "Would you still like that story?"

"I would love a distraction," I agreed, needing time to process my feelings before going back to the guys.

He looked off like he was consulting his bank of memories, then got into a story that painted my grandmother in a completely different light than when I knew her; the Evelyn only Charlie told me about. I loved how he made Grams strong and fierce, always standing up for people.

"She chained herself to a tree? Literally?" I verified after his third story, this one about her protesting so they wouldn't cut down a tree on their university campus.

"She was part of a nature conservation group and tried to make it a landmark, but the truth of it was that she couldn't care less about what kind of tree it was or how long it was there. Your grandfather had just passed away, and when we were at school together, he carved their initials into the tree and vowed to love her forever."

"She was saving the memories…I guess that's when she started being a shut-in?"

"She was as carefree and headstrong as ever," he argued. "Laurel and I were in town when it happened, so once the tree was safe, we took her out to dinner, and she was every bit as sharp and full of plans and ideas as she ever was."

"I thought she became afraid of people and leaving home after my grandfather died?"

"No, that was months later."

"When it hit her?" Grief had many stages before acceptance.

"No, it didn't have anything to do with Grant, I don't think," he said of my grandfather.

"Was there something else to explain it? Or did she just wake up one day and decide she didn't want to go outside anymore?" I found the whole thing ridiculous, but I understood that loss made people do crazy things.

"No one ever told you?" Charlie shifted awkwardly, for the first time since we started talking, probably an hour ago.

"Told me what?"

"She stopped going out around the time your mom had you."

"It was because of me?"

"It had nothing to do with you, sweetie, Evelyn loved you to the moon and back," he assured me.

"But…" I pressed.

"Your father," he admitted.

"You know who my father is?" I was shocked. Every time I asked, it was implied that my mom and dad weren't all that serious, she never brought him home, and he bailed as soon as he found out she was pregnant.

"Maybe this isn't the right conversation to be getting your mind off things."

"I don't mean to put you on the spot, but no one ever talks about my father. I didn't think anyone knew who he was." My father was listed as Unknown in the Chronicles. Even Henry was named as Margaret's father, even if it didn't mention his exploits.

"It really isn't my place to tell you." Charlie was apologetic, but wouldn't give me more answers.

"And the people whose place it is would rather keep me in the dark and pretend they're protecting me." We were back at square one. "I'm sorry, that wasn't aimed at—"

"Are you okay?" Charlie asked, leaning in, and putting his hand on my shoulder when I suddenly stopped talking.

"I'm fine," I assured him, feeling the hairs on the back of my neck stick up. "Do you think you and Eric could stay somewhere else tonight? Like maybe Ingrid's?" I asked.

"Eric's already on his way back to his dorm. What's going on?"

"Someone is coming here looking for me, and I don't want you to be here when he finds me."

"Why are you still here?" he asked me.

"Because it'll never end if I keep running."

He looked like he wanted to argue, but the look in my eyes must have convinced him. "I'll see you in the morning." He set his jaw, but I could see his eyes tearing up.

"Thank you. For everything." I hoped I would make it through, but this time I planned on being strong like Annabelle, if ever it came down to it.

"Be careful," he told me before going home, while I headed for Embry's villa to prepare for battle.

CHAPTER TWENTY-SEVEN

Embry and Gabriel were sitting in the kitchen with a rather large sword and an axe on the table between them. You could cut the tension with a knife, but for once it wasn't aimed at each other.

"Can I get you anything?" I expected them to yell at me for running off when Donovan was on his way, but Embry showed nothing but concern for my well-being.

"I'm fine," I said, looking from one to the other.

For a minute, the three of us stood there, no one really knowing what to say.

"I'm sorry," they both blurted out at the same time.

"We never knew that he cared about your birthmark. We always assumed he wanted you because you were his descendants," Gabriel came clean, honestly answering the question I asked months ago, when I found out about the Prophecy.

"Did the other Bearers of the Crescent Moon find out who was hunting them?" I asked.

"Cass…" Embry said before they exchanged a look. I gave them one as well, so they decided to share. "She came face to face with him and he made her think he didn't want to hurt her, or her daughter, because they were his blood. She didn't tell us everything he said, there wasn't time, but he used it to trick her."

"Wouldn't it make sense to warn me ahead of time, so I wouldn't fall for his tricks?" I suggested.

"In retrospect...maybe. But I saw what it did to Beth when she found out, and I couldn't put that on you." Embry put his hand on mine, seeking forgiveness, while Gabriel's eyes widened with the knowledge that Embry told Beth. I was glad he meant it when he told me they had no secrets.

"Donovan is in New Orleans." I brought us back to the matter at hand.

"The car is packed..." Embry tried one last time, but I shook my head.

"If you absolutely want to take our chances against Donovan..." Gabriel paused, his eyes pleading for me to change my mind. "We have weapons," he said, taking the axe.

"You need to listen to us though, Lucy. If I tell you to run to the panic room, you need to run to the panic room," Embry warned.

"I'm not going to abandon the two of you to face him when you wanted to take me away," I argued.

"Will you at least hide?" he tried instead.

"What's your plan?" Gabriel gave me a chance.

"From what I gather, you guys keep coming back as long as your body isn't damaged beyond repair. There are cases of severed heads being sewn back on..." I blinked hard to get the image out of my mind. "But I don't think you can come back from what I did to that woman."

"You want to blow him up?" Embry raised his eyebrows at me.

"I want to stop him from hurting more people I care about. If we can tie him up and lock him in the panic room for all eternity, I'm good with that too."

"What if things get out of hand? He brings an army, and we

can't handle it?" Gabriel asked with a warning look, as if he knew my plan.

"I'll run to the panic room." I partially meant it. Depending on what he came at us with, it might be better for Donovan and I to be locked in the panic room. Powers work on the inside, but they can't get out to hurt anyone else.

THE GUYS HAD both spent time as soldiers, so they seemed perfectly content to wait for Donovan to show up. I, on the other hand, was a pack of nerves. I felt like I should be practicing or learning more techniques or…anything would be better than nothing. I had the vials of potion I made with Ingrid, but wasn't sure what would be useful. Donovan could control other Gifted, and I assumed he had magical powers, but it wasn't like he was going to be poisoning me or drinking anything I gave him. That left me with the focusing draught. I held the tiny bottle up to the light, wondering if potions went bad, when the guys stood up, alert.

"Someone's here," Embry explained as they positioned themselves between me and the door. There was a loud noise, the screech of metal on pavement, before we all recognized Ingrid's voice in the backyard.

"He's close." She gave an involuntary shudder as she came into the kitchen and gave Embry a hug.

"How do you know?" Gabriel asked.

"Charlie came to my place and said you might need some help," she explained her arrival. "And I can feel his magic." Another shiver. I thought it was because I did the tracking spell earlier, but if she felt it too…

"Can you tell how powerful he is?" Embry asked before his eyes darted to the ceiling, but I didn't hear anything.

"A lot stronger than I am." She hugged herself, then shook it off. "That was him?"

"He's on the property," Embry agreed.

"It's now or never my dear, he's here." Ingrid nodded encouragingly to the vial, so I knocked it back and braced myself.

I was grateful Embry chose to bring us out to the yard instead of waiting in the house for Donovan. It felt good to move. Even if we were exposed out here in the open, it was better than feeling caged inside.

More than anything, I wanted to wrap a force shield around the four of us, but Donovan might not know about my powers, and I didn't want to show him all my cards.

"Pretty brave, choosing her house." Donovan walked over to us as calmly as if we were old friends meeting in the park.

Embry, Gabriel, and Ingrid stood facing him like statues while I felt like I was made of Jell-O. Or something crumblier.

"Where's Richard?" Donovan sounded bored.

"You didn't stab him with a tracker as well?" Gabriel stepped forward, more so he could adjust his position to cover me than out of bravery.

"His went dark." Donovan didn't look the least bit concerned about Richard's well-being, but the lack of information was a mild annoyance.

Embry must have heard my breath catch in my chest because he reached a hand back to take mine. I hadn't asked about the jogger because I didn't want to know what 'whatever it takes' meant.

"Lucy." Donovan's focus turned to me. "I have a proposition for you."

"Do you want me to rule by Henry's side again?" I used his name, but got no reaction.

"Oh, I think that ship has sailed." His smile was downright

jovial, which terrified me. "This one might be better suited for you."

"You had my brother killed. If I didn't take your offer when his life was in the balance, there is nothing you could say or do to make me willingly consider your offer now." I knew I was stalling, but I had a sudden appreciation for why villains always shared their evil plans before putting them into action on TV.

"I admit I was wrong in assuming you would sacrifice yourself to save someone you love." Donovan paused to look at me, his words making my blood boil. "But what about saving yourself?"

Sam's death replayed in my mind, and Donovan's implications brought an anger like I had never felt before. I tried to steady my breathing, but it was no use.

"Argh!" I screamed, making a guttural sound that shocked me, as I sent a blast of energy at him. Donovan was caught off guard for a moment, so the blast pushed him back a couple of feet before he tossed it to the side, barely even losing his footing.

"My, how the generations have diluted your magic." Donovan chuckled to himself before sending a green orb at us. I conjured a force shield, but instead of bouncing off, the green orb pushed against my shield, digging its way in like Mr. Fraser tried to do to my mind. It took Ingrid putting her hand on my shoulder to help me push the orb off.

I HAD BEEN PRAYING Donovan would come alone, without an army, because I truly thought we could defeat him. We outnumbered him, and everyone insisted my magic was powerful, so I believed them. Even holding on to the moonstone and to Ingrid's hand did nothing more than put dents in Donovan's metaphorical armor. I threw everything I had at him, trying to protect

Embry and Gabriel as they faced him with their medieval weapons. If we managed to coordinate our attacks, he would go slightly off-balance, but I was the only one who could get close enough to him without risking being controlled. If four against one was giving us trouble, three against two would destroy us.

INGRID WAS the first to fall. She tried altering Donovan's perception of reality, but it was like he could sense the guys once they got close enough, and he had no qualms about haphazardly sending blasts of energy and sparks in every direction. Even if he couldn't see where we were, he still had a pretty good chance of hitting one of us. And unless something substantial stopped them, his curses were endless, which put everyone in the neighborhood at risk.

Eventually, Donovan sent one of his green orbs at Embry, then immediately sent one at us. I had already conjured a force shield to protect Embry from the brunt of the blast, so I couldn't conjure another one fast enough. Ingrid tried to use her magic to send the orb back to Donovan, but she only managed to slow it down before it hit her square in the chest.

In the time it took me to get to Ingrid and see that the blow was fatal, Donovan had already frozen Gabriel's axe midair and reached out to touch him.

Time froze, or at least I could swear my heart stopped as Gabriel's expression went from shock to a blank slate to determination as Donovan took over his mind. Gabriel turned away from Donovan, set his sights on me, and pounced.

I had my hands ready to conjure a force shield, but Embry cut in between us before I had to find out if I could have gone through with fighting Gabriel to save myself.

"Get out of here Lucy," Embry called to me, every blow between him and Gabriel constricting my heart tighter, the sound of metal on metal so much worse than nails on a chalkboard could ever be.

DODGING orbs and blasts had brought me closer to the stables than to the villa, with Donovan and Gabriel between me and the panic room, as well as the getaway car.

I stepped back slowly as Donovan made his way towards me. He wasn't sending anything at me, but he had his hands at the ready. I was convinced he would stop me if I tried to run.

"Have you reconsidered?" Donovan asked, wiping a bead of sweat from his brow. It was good to know that our defense was exerting him, if nothing else.

"I want nothing to do with you." I calculated my chances of escaping on horseback to be somewhere around zero.

"I'm not sure you understand. Turning me down means you die within the decade. No matter what."

"I'll take my chances." I stood as tall as I possibly could, to show him I meant it and he didn't scare me, even though he did.

"Then you leave me no choice." For a moment, he stood there, palms facing upwards, shaking his head at me. The next, he had covered the distance between us and wrapped his surprisingly strong hands around my tiny, fragile neck. I tried to freeze him, to buy myself some time, but nothing worked. I couldn't stop him, levitate him, move him away from me, or bring anything over. I was helpless.

I screamed, using my hands to try and release his grip, but the weight of him brought me down to the floor. My lungs were aching for air, but all I could think was that I couldn't let him take my heart.

Embry had mentioned that there were places on the property where Gifts and magic didn't work. This was either one of them, or I had exhausted all my powers. Since Donovan was on top of me, strangling me instead of using his magic, I assumed I wasn't the problem. I tried to rip his fingers off my throat or push him away, but it didn't work. I was no match for him, so I dropped my arms. I thought I had given up, but my body had other plans. My hands travelled along the ground, searching for something they could save me with, and found a rock. I lifted it up and brought it smashing into Donovan's skull.

I think he was more frazzled than hurt, but it still gave me the chance to get up and run to the big barn doors. He followed me, like I knew he would, but I just needed to get far enough ahead of him for my magic to come back. It was the only logical explanation, and if I was wrong, I was dead anyway.

I didn't feel anything when I crossed the threshold, but I turned to face Donovan with my hands on the moonstone necklace. I closed my eyes and channeled everything I had into blasting him into oblivion. I felt like my soul was drained into the magic as I fell to my knees, too scared to open my eyes.

I took a deep breath and found the spot where I last saw Donovan, half-expecting him to give me one last menacing smile before carting me off to Henry, but he was gone. In his place, there was nothing but a pile of ash.

CHAPTER TWENTY-EIGHT

"Lucy!" I heard my name, but it sounded so far away. I was cold and damp, which didn't make any sense, until I opened my eyes and saw that I was lying in the dew-covered grass in front of the barn. It was early morning, though I don't think I was out longer than a few minutes. I still felt so tired.

I saw Embry and tried to stand, to run to him, but everything around me started spinning. I would have fallen back onto the grass if Gabriel hadn't appeared out of nowhere and caught me.

"You're friends again?" I verified, judging by the fact that he wasn't trying to kill me.

"You did it, Lucy. Donovan can't hurt you anymore." Gabriel looked at me with…not quite incredulity, but definitely amazement and respect.

"The ashes…" I turned, pointing to the pile of what used to be Donovan.

"We'll take care of them," Embry assured me. "You're safe."

"We need to get out of here," I argued, walking towards the villa. Henry might not sit back and wait for us to find him if he knew exactly where we were. "We are nowhere near safe."

"No, we're not," Embry agreed. "But you accomplished something huge, and we need to—"

"We need more magic," I cut him off. "If Henry is more powerful than Donovan, we don't stand a chance. We can't let him complete the ritual. There would be no stopping him." Part of me always thought they were exaggerating, but the four of us barely managed to defeat Donovan, and that was without an army of supernatural minions to contend with.

"We can look into it and figure something out." Embry gave me an encouraging smile.

"Those books in the bunker that you didn't want to fall into the wrong hands…" I pried.

"They might be worth a look," Gabriel agreed.

"Will Ingrid be okay?" I asked once I got to her, kneeling down to bring her head into my lap. With her illusions gone, she looked like a sleeping child.

"She should wake up in a few hours," Embry assured me. "We can bring her to Charlie's so he can keep an eye on her."

"And Richard?" I used the name Donovan gave us, trying to stay composed.

"The child was returned to his mother and Richard spent the night, alive, in a very special mausoleum. He'll be back with his family and able to destroy us in no time." Gabriel didn't look happy about it, but I believed him.

"We should leave before that happens," Embry suggested.

THE GUYS WENT to burn Donovan's ashes while I carried Ingrid onto a couch in Charlie's living room. I stayed by her side and held her hand, knowing there was no way I could ever repay what she'd done for me. Or get over the sight of her lying lifeless on the grass.

"Charlie's back. It's time to go." Gabriel came to warn me as I was running my fingers through Ingrid's hair like I used to do for Clara.

"I'll be right there." I waited until he was gone to place a kiss on her forehead.

I ran into Mr. Fraser on my way out and hesitated, not sure if she would want him to see her like that, but someone must have called him.

"I've got her," he promised me, fighting to keep it together.

"Tell her…" I paused, trying to find the words to convey my love and admiration for her. "Tell her it has been an honor learning and fighting alongside her."

He nodded, clearing his throat, then went to Ingrid's side. I watched as he tenderly brushed the hair from her forehead, then went to join the guys at the villa.

THE CAR WAS MOSTLY PACKED, so the guys put their weapons in the trunk, and I took Ingrid's potions. The villa had come to feel like home, but we wouldn't stand a chance against Henry if he came after us now. I'd put everyone in danger long enough.

"I told you I would see you in the morning." Relief was etched all over Charlie's face as he left Embry to come and take me in for a hug.

"Thank you for the help," I told him, trying not to cry, but something about him was making me tear up.

"I'm always here. Always willing to lend a hand," he assured me as Embry got into the driver's seat, letting me know it was time to go. "This isn't how I would have wanted you to find out, but I know you have to leave, and I don't want to be another person keeping things from you."

"What are you talking about?" I asked before remembering last night's conversation. It felt like lifetimes ago.

"This is all I know about it. But sometimes it's better to leave good enough alone." Charlie put an envelope in my hand, then covered it with both of his. "You take care now."

"You too." I took him in for a hug, then got into the back seat.

I waved to Charlie as we pulled out of the driveway, looking back until I couldn't see him or the property anymore. Our general direction was home, but the home from my memories was gone. Nothing in my life would ever be anything like it was before. But in spite of our crushing near-defeat, I felt hope. Yes, it took everything from us to defeat Donovan and we barely made it out alive, but Gifted weren't invincible and hopefully, neither was Henry.

Find out how Lucy's story ends in
Legacy (The Owens Chronicles Book Three)
***

Keep reading for a bonus scene with
Gabriel, Rosalind, and Molly!

BONUS SCENE

A FEW MONTHS AFTER GABRIEL FIRST MEETS ROSALIND

When Gabriel was finally well enough to leave the plantation's makeshift hospital, he was nowhere near ready to say goodbye.

"I guess you'll be heading out tomorrow," Rosalind said when he took his thrice-daily walk around the floor.

"That's what they tell me," he agreed, instead of admitted how badly he wanted to stay.

"You can finally go find your Annabelle," she said nervously, waiting for his reaction.

"What?" He'd been asking himself if staying here and pretending Rosalind was Annabelle was something he could do.

"When you first woke up, you called me Annabelle," she explained. "You can go be with her now."

"Annabelle died many years ago," he admitted. "Perhaps I believed I had woken up in heaven. I would love nothing more than to be with her, but I'm afraid there must be something I have to do here first."

"I'm so sorry." Maybe that's what she recognized in him, the pain that was so piercing in her own heart. "My husband, I pretend he'll be coming home, for Molly's sake as well as my

231

own, but I know, deep down, that he's dead. That I won't see him again until I die as well."

"Some loves outlast life, death, and all worldly conventions," he let her know he understood.

"Where is home for you?"

He couldn't exactly say that he had grown up here, in a house down the road. That he enjoyed many meals at the table they now used for operations, and played in the very fields and creeks her daughter was out discovering as they spoke. Instead, he made up a lie, convincingly telling her of a childhood and a family in a different town. Another world.

"You must be anxious to get back to them." There was something behind her kindness that worried him, the hint that she didn't want him to leave either.

"No, it's just me," he argued. Any family he'd had died many lifetimes ago. All he had left of that life was Embry, and they were far from being on speaking terms. Last he heard, Embry was back in Italy, pretending to be his own grandson.

"You could stay," she offered, and if she had meant just as another patient, or as a friend, he would have done it. He would have spent the next ten or even twenty years there, until people became suspicious of his youth and forced him to move on.

But Rosalind looked at him like she was lonely, and he was kind, and her daughter enjoyed his company, as did she. No matter how much he wished he could, he loved Annabelle, not just for the way she looked, but for everything inside of her that made her his soul mate.

"I'm afraid my duty is to my country." He hoped he sounded convincing, though he had never felt a strong patriotism, or the need to defend any country. There were things he would lay down his life for without hesitation, but they were people, not governments or ideals.

"My husband's was as well." She gave him a sad smile.

"I'll probably leave early. Long before your day begins, so I would thank you now for your hospitality, and for taking care of me," he said, knowing he wouldn't be able to go through this again.

"It was my pleasure," she assured him, failing to hide the disappointment. "If it isn't too much trouble, do try to let Molly say goodbye before you leave. She is quite fond of you, and she's had enough men leave without proper goodbyes."

Rosalind said her piece and left in a hurry, as if she had a patient or work to tend to.

It would be easier for him to just leave now, while no one was watching, and disappear into the night, but he obliged Rosalind's last request. He found Molly under the stairs, where he knew she liked to read when the house got too busy.

"What do we have here?" he asked, slipping into the tiny room under the stairs and closing the door, so it was just the two of them.

"Mama wrote it for me. It's about a little girl who is strong and almost never afraid, so she goes on adventures."

"Sounds lovely," he assured her, noting yet another difference between the two women who looked alike. Rosalind wrote stories, whereas Annabelle had sung to get her daughter to sleep, claiming she had absolutely no imagination for things like that.

"We can read it together if you like," Molly offered, her smile widening and breaking his heart a little in the process.

"I'm afraid I'll be leaving very early in the morning. I came to say goodbye."

"Because you're all better, so you have to go home?" She seemed determine not to show her emotions.

"That is the way it goes," he said instead of admitting how much he wished he could stay.

"And it has to be tomorrow?" she asked like it was just out of curiosity, not because she was going to miss him.

"My men need me," he said of the imaginary soldiers he was supposed to be fighting with. Lately, he had mostly been wandering the countryside on his own, joining battles as he encountered them.

"Then I hope you have a safe journey." Molly did her best not to cry, and his heart swelled with pride, and how much he was going to miss this little girl.

"You as well my dear." He nodding to her book and got up.

"Gabriel…" she called him back when he had his hand on the door, about to walk out.

"Yes, sweetie?" He mentally cursed himself for the term of endearment that would just make things harder for both of them.

"Would you mind reading with me before you go, just for a bit? There are some words I'm not sure I understand."

He knew she could read well above her age, but he accepted the excuse as if he believed it, and sat down on the pile of pillows with her.

"Of course." He picked up the book and read as if his heart wasn't aching.

At first, Molly read over his shoulder, correcting him when he purposely made a mistake to test her, but eventually, she fell asleep with her head resting on his shoulder. After a half an hour or so, when he could no longer pretend he didn't know she was sleeping, he gently lifted her off his shoulder, and tucked her under a quilt.

Once she was settled, he ever so gently kissed her head, and left them both behind, refusing to look back.

ACKNOWLEDGMENTS

To my mom, who from Day One has been my biggest fan and supporter. She helps me with revision after revision and lets me bounce all of my ideas off her. I literally couldn't do it without you. I love you so much. Thank you.

To my grandmother, who can't read my books because they put her to sleep, but loves me unconditionally. She feeds my soul with love and laughter, and my stomach with her delicious baking. You are the glue that holds this family together and I owe you so much of my happiness. xo

To Liz, who offered to Beta read and became a pseudo-editor. Thank you for your guidance and advice. I appreciate it from the bottom of my heart and owe you one. Or many.

To Rikki, who took the time to give me her feedback in an honest and supportive way. It means the world to have someone care so fiercely about my characters.

To everyone who made this book a reality, THANK YOU!

P.S. I finished this book during a pandemic, which was quite an experience. Some days the writing came easy, and on others I kept the document open without writing a word. So I want to thank the people who called, who wrote, who cared. The ones who created content or ran in a penguin costume to lift people's spirits. Who shared baby pictures when we needed a smile. Who took my mind off things with zoom calls, trivia nights, and wii golf. Who sat with me and escaped through movies. You provided me with a happy place in scary times and I am grateful.

GIFTEDVERSE

AMANDA LYNN
PETRIN

LEGACY

THE OWENS CHRONICLES
BOOK THREE

CHAPTER TWO

EXCERPT

"Is there anything you would like to tell me about all the Crescent Moon Bearers?" I asked, focusing on Gabriel.

"What?" he sounded confused.

"Is there something about Annabelle, Rosalind, Cassandra, and Elizabeth that one of you should have told me by now?" I rephrased my question, turning to Embry. He used to be the one to tell me things, once upon a time. My eyes were glistening, but I refused to blink and let the tears fall.

"We have centuries of knowledge on your family, Lucy, we obviously can't have told you everything." Embry was getting worried, but neither of them seemed to know what I was getting at.

"How old was Annabelle when she died?" I asked Gabriel.

"Twenty-eight," he said like it still stung.

"And how old was Beth?" A shiver went through me from the memory, still so fresh in my mind, and my skin. I skipped the others and stuck to the two that affected them the most.

"Twenty-eight." I could see Embry's brain working, doing the same math for Cassie and Rosie. "But that's…" he tried to reason it away.

"It's not a coincidence that Beth was trampled, suffocated, and burnt alive at the same age as Annabelle," I argued. "Cassie and Rosie were also twenty-eight." I handed him the Chronicles.

"We knew they died young, but… No one gave Rosie tuberculosis. Annabelle chose to sacrifice herself for Margaret. And no one could have predicted the lighting room would catch fire. It's just a coincidence," Embry tried to convince himself.

"I thought the Universe sent you guys to protect me, not that I would die either way." I shook my head and stared out the window.

"No, there is no curse on you, no other prophecy, nothing that implies the same will happen to you," Gabriel argued like he wouldn't accept the alternative.

"Except for precedence and the lack of a single exception." I wanted to throw up. "Stop the car," I said evenly, clenching my jaw to stop the tears.

"Luce," Embry tried to talk me down.

"I need some air," I pleaded. "Whether or not you accept it, there's a distinct possibility, that even if Henry never gets to me, some force out there will make sure I never make it to thirty, and right now I can't breathe." I aggressively rolled down the window. "You guys help me survive and make it through all the attempts to kill me, but maybe you're just here so they can't complete the ritual. Because that's the endgame. You help me survive as long as I can, then make sure Henry doesn't get my body when it happens?" I felt sick.

"That's not how it is," Embry argued.

"Neither of us is resigned to you dying. And if his plan wasn't to kill you, I would rather you be with Henry than be dead," Gabriel said, the vein in his forehead pulsing as he tried to control his emotions and the car.

I would call him on his lie by telling him I knew they would kill me themselves rather than let Henry do what he had to with me, but when his eyes met mine… I believed him.

"Whether you like it or not, I will die when I'm twenty-eight, won't I?" I stopped being angry and turned vulnerable, which felt worse.

"It's a possibility," Embry said after considering it.

"That we will do absolutely everything in our power to make sure doesn't happen," Gabriel assured me.

"Please stop the car." The numbness in my voice scared me, which is probably why Gabriel pulled onto the shoulder. The child lock was still on the doors, so I looked over to him. His eyes were pleading with me not to go, but he pushed the button to let me out. I shut the door and walked towards the wooded area beside the highway.

I looked back to see them looking after me before I kept going, past the tree line, into the dense parts where the remaining bits of sun struggled to get in. It was only once I could no longer hear the cars that I truly let the implications hit me. No matter what anyone did, within ten years, I would be dead. I brought my hand up to run my fingers through my hair, an attempt at self-soothing, but ended up pressing my hand to my forehead as a searing pain shot through my skull.

Find out how Lucy's story ends in
Legacy (The Owens Chronicles Book Three)

www.ingramcontent.com/pod-product-compliance
Lightning Source LLC
Chambersburg PA
CBHW021130190726
48288CB00008B/2588